NIGHTMARE WORLD

Stack hissed as the herd of rats ran between and around the wheels, some moving out in front of the van while others climbed up the sides, their nails clicking across the roof and windows. Rat climbing over rat; rat holding onto rat until the deadly gray carpet quickly covered every square inch.

As he sat there, trapped and watching, rats swarmed over the van, looking for a way in. Yellowed fangs, gnashing teeth, open, pink-tongued mouths, bristly whiskers, red, beady eyes: they were ready to bite into his flesh, moving this way and that, sniffing for a way in. Stack could almost smell their hot, fetid breath. It made his skin crawl. He had to get out of there!

The ROADBLASTER series:
#1 Hell Ride

DEATH RIDE

Paul Hofrichter

LEISURE BOOKS NEW YORK CITY

I would like to dedicate this story to Leslie Marianko, who graciously read and commented on two previous works of mine, and I would also like to thank Abe Horowitz (a.k.a. Al Ragu) who was there at all times to ably repair the machines with which I turn out my work.

A LEISURE BOOK

Published by

Dorchester Publishing Co., Inc.
6 East 39th Street
New York, NY 10016

Printed in the United States of America

1

Nick Stack was 16 again. High school felt so good. It was all so real that he felt he could reach out and touch the peeling walls in the long, cool, dark halls. He could feel each jolt along the balls of his feet and the length of his legs as he took the stairs two at a time racing down the broad concrete steps in front of Christopher Columbus High School, as he ran to the sidewalk past the high, black gates that looked like hundreds of metal spears set upright on long metal racks. In his flashback, Stack watched himself dodging the crowd, missing clumps of students who stood together smoking, joking, shrieking with laughter; the guys eyeing the girls, who eyed them back, each of them talking about this or that date, teacher, or test.

Nick Stack bubbled over with life, enthusiasm, and the exuberance of youth, stopping along the way to talk to various friends, bumming a cigarette off one boy, moving aside as one of the school tough guys headed for the curb where out-of-school guys had pulled in with their hot rod, which had a bright metal bar across the back of the front seat with the words Fool Injection painted on the bar in black paint. The guys in the car looked like they were waiting for the better pieces to come out of school so they could take them for a ride, perhaps out to Orchard Beach, where they could kiss, get some feels, and maybe for the luckier ones—sex.

Nick spotted a girl he had been trying to go out with. Lydia. Wide-hipped, with great legs and a fine backside that always turned him on. He called her name. She stopped, turned around, and gave him a steady grin, always glad to see Nick and talk to him. He went over, put his arm around her shoulders, and held her as they walked along, Nick smiling at Lydia, his heart beating a bit too fast, though he seemed nonchalant on the surface, as if this were natural for him and he did it all the time. He wished that were so. Lydia felt so good to hold and walk with, so right in his arms, that he wanted to keep her by him forever, smiling into her face, fantasizing about taking her to Orchard Beach and there, in the bushes back from the beach, hidden from prying eyes, enjoying her the way he had always dreamed.

But the dream, which is all it was, began to dissipate like gossamer as deeper, darker currents welled up from some greater depth and with a jolt he came awake, his heart beating too fast. Not the rapid pounding that comes during good sex, but the racing thumps of fear, of the hunted fleeing the hunter. And this time Nick Stack really was the hunted. He swallowed and shook his head, suddenly aware of the exhaustion which had allowed him to briefly fall asleep in the front of the sheriff's police cruiser as he sat waiting for the driver to return.

Quickly, Nick Stack remembered where he was, what he had done, and where he was going. His mind focused for long seconds on the wisps of the dream before wakefulness caused it all to flee from his memory. He smiled grimly at a world that had been and now was no more. That had been 20 years ago. Two decades of hard living. A past as unreal as his present and future were now.

Lydia. The name dropped from his lips like ruby red wine. Where was she now? Was she married, with children, and still alive? That too he could not answer.

He shook his head to clear it. It was a new day, but there was no hope in the deceptively clear air. Less than 48 hours earlier Russia and America had engaged in a fierce nuclear exchange which devastated military bases and the larger cities, leaving the open spaces between metropolises largely untouched except for the deadly clouds of radiation now passing across the terrain. Lethal enough to kill in some places, mild enough to make people sick for hours or days in other locations, slowly dissipating as they did their ruthless work. Stack and many others had come down with the radiation sickness and were now just recovering. He wondered if it would happen again and how soon. For this question, as well as many others, he had no answers.

A fairly muscular man with black hair and liquid brown eyes in a tanned, round face, Stack lit a cigarette and smoked absentmindedly as he looked around for Sheriff Kurt Willem, the only law in the town of Montieth, where they were supposed to go soon.

Stack pushed his mind back 48 hours to when he had found himself in the middle of a surprise war while camping in the wilderness of north central California on a long-needed vacation. He thought about the people he had met in the short time that had followed the outbreak of war and turned men's souls inside out.

The first had been Rayisa Gilchrist, 14, with reddish, shoulder-length hair, freckles, and long, coltish legs. He had given her a lift when she'd tried to get from her aunt's home in the mountains to Fresno, where she'd lived. But now that city and most of its inhabitants, including her parents, were gone. Rayisa had been kidnapped by a gang of motorcycle toughs and ordered to perform sex on one of them. But she'd been rescued at the last moment by Stack, who'd been forced by events to become hero of the hour. This had been followed by a run-in with the bikers, who'd taken the town of Vista Royale hostage. Stack was there now. The town had been saved, though not before Stack, Willem, and a host of others had spent a hard night in a nearby valley saving a B-52 bomber, loaded with hydrogen bombs, from being taken over by the motorcycle gang. The gang would have used the bomber's deadly weapons to threaten the survivors in the mountains, becoming their supreme masters. The B-52 had landed at the deserted airfield because of mechanical difficulties which kept it from dropping its bombs over Siberia.

Stack was proud of what he and the others had done. But he also wanted to be back in Montieth, where Rayisa was staying at a friend's house. He wanted to be there when she awoke from the sedative the doctor had given her so she could recuperate from the shock of what had happened the previous evening. The war, her kidnapping, the forced sex, the rescue, and the death she saw were more than what one girl should have to undergo. However, across the globe various people were being forced to undergo various hells not of their making and over which they had only minimal control. Rayisa's tragedy was just one in a long litany of tragedies which had struck and would strike people everywhere.

And tragedy was no stranger to Stack either. He was trapped in California, while his wife, two sons, daughter, brother, and father were in New York City, 3000 miles across the nation on the other side of the continent. And who knew if they were even alive? But Stack forced that from his mind. He would take only one obstacle at a time. Thinking too far ahead was dangerous. There lay the road to madness.

He finished his cigarette, tossed it out the open window, and watched it spark on the asphalt of the road, the sparks flying off on an early morning wind thick with the pine freshness of the surrounding forests, which washed like a giant green sea across the surrounding mountain peaks. Stack inhaled the freshness, closed his eyes a moment, and asked himself the same question he had asked since the war had begun. How much radiation filled the fresh wind and the forested glades and the sky overhead? He didn't know, and that too bothered him. Stack was overwhelmed by endless waves of problems, obstacles, doubts and worries. There seemed no end to them. And each was bigger than the one before. He felt like a wooden ship on an endless ocean and reacted more than acted against negative stimuli.

But that too was forgotten as he half turned in his seat and saw Willem coming from the town hall. They'd been feted and thanked at an early-morning breakfast. Many of the men who'd help save the town and the bomber were staying to help Vista Royale reorganize and bury the dead. The rest were guarding the bomber. But Willem and Stack had a date in Montieth.

The big, thick sheriff opened the door and slid in behind the wheel. He gave Stack a tight little smile, showing tobacco-yellowed teeth and a thin mustache framing a small, worried mouth in a ham-sized and ham-shaped face.

Willem started the car. The motor roared to life and caused the vehicle to vibrate. Then they were off, heading out of town along a deserted road cutting through the mountain wilderness to Montieth, some 40 miles away.

The two men did not talk much. Both had plenty to think over and worry about. Stack looked at himself briefly in the mirror mounted on his door and saw the tense look on his face and the glint of panic in his eyes. Eyes that were much too bright. But this he could not control. He had read somewhere that the eyes were the mirror of the soul. And these eyes mirrored the fear inside, the turmoil he barely held in check, the tumult of events, the bits and pieces of his past now coming to the surface. It was almost as if all the hells he'd undergone over the last two days were now coming to the fore. Before that he'd been too busy fighting his own and other people's battles. And when a man's fighting he can't worry about what's coming down the road tomorrow, or the next set of tomorrows. There isn't time to reflect. But now he had the time, and the worry just wouldn't stop.

For a few seconds he felt shivers running up and down his spine. Not now, he told himself. There was too much to do. Too many puzzles to solve. Too many dilemmas to avoid. Too many people who needed his help and needed it badly. Stack would have to forget about his insides and fight the battles which loomed ahead. Others had done it before him. He could do it now.

Stack thought again about his family and wondered if they were still alive. Somehow he had to get out of these mountains and catch a plane back to New York City. He thought of the B-52 and decided to find out if the crew would do him the favor and take him to New York. They had the fuel and the range. And if not New York, then someplace in between where another plane could be caught going east. It sounded like a silly fantasy, an impossible dream. But somewhere planes and airfields had survived. Stack would not give up. He'd talk with the B-52 crew, find out what they intended to do and where they planned to go. After all, they wouldn't just sit there. Flyers were men of action.

The trip went faster this time around. Shorter than it had seemed the night before when they'd come this way from Montieth. And then, before he knew it, Montieth loomed up suddenly along the road, reminding him of the first time he had come here with Rayisa beside him.

Montieth was difficult to spot at first because the houses on this end of town were of unpainted lumber or of log construction and blended in with the surrounding forest, so that one was almost into Montieth before seeing that the highway also doubled as Main Street, lined on both sides with stores and houses, mostly of wood, some of brick, none over two stories high. Then one spotted the side-streets, roads moving up or down sloping ground, and around it all the hulking green carpet of the forest with the backdrop of distant mountains, gray granite peaks pointing up from the convoluted green mass growing along sharp-sided flanks.

Willem slowed down as they got into Montieth. Ladies from the church still had their refreshment stand off to one side, across from a small playground park, to feed travelers staggering in from who knew where. The women behind the table, little old ladies with blue dyed hair, looked like the reception committee at a church picnic. The smiles on their faces were more forced than two days ago. Anxious smiles. Inquiring smiles. The horror of what had gone on with the bombings and the lawlessness across the land was only now sinking in.

The table they had set up still held plenty of food. There was a number of stragglers around it. And kids still played in the small park across the street. Yet there was a more pessimistic mood in the air than there had been just after the war broke out. The first cases of radiation sickness had been experienced, and were only now being recovered from. So far, this area had been lucky, getting only a light dose as the winds dissipated the coastal mushroom clouds. However, there would be more radiation, and no one could predict how lethal a dose the next wind pattern would bring.

Willem stopped the car as a small crowd gathered, and told the people how the motorcycle gang had been defeated in Vista Royale and that those who weren't killed had fled the scene. He then related how the B-52 had been saved and the people cheered, glad that this menace had been banished from the mountains. But at the time there was an undertone of worry, the darker lining in their silver cloud.

Willem started the car, yelled out that he had business elsewhere, and slowly moved forward as the crowd dissipated. Nor did they have far to go. Montieth was not a big place. Perhaps 600 souls in all. More of an extended family than anything else.

Willem did not drive immediately to the Winston house, where Rayisa was staying, but stopped on a sidestreet close to the woods. The two men looked around. No one was outside. It was almost like a Sunday morning before church.

They lit cigarettes and sat there, smoking a few moments in silence, then began to talk. Willem first.

"I don't like the mood in town."

"It'll get worse. If it stayed at this level I wouldn't mind.

There's plenty of trouble ahead."

"You mean radiation?"

"That's the least of it. How long do you think the food supply will last? A few days before what's in people's homes is gone. Then they'll hit the food shops. If there's no hoarding by the owners—and the law, meaning yourself, will have to insure that—the food should last a few days more. Since nobody's delivering anything, people will have to go down to the farmers near here. And, if the farmers are willing to sell, they'll be able to get items at inflated prices. Some corn, some wheat—which will have to be milled, some chickens perhaps, and so on. Not a very appealing diet. I'm afraid the Russkis have it all over us in that department. They're used to eating a less plentiful, harsher diet."

"Yeah," Willem said, reflecting deeply as he took another pull on his cigarette. "Luckily we had a long-distance trucker with nowhere to go, who stopped here with a trailer of refrigerated meat that he let us have."

"And how long will that last? Four, five days when the town has nothing left to eat. The people of Montieth can go through a ton a day. Two, three pounds per person per day over three meals. And that's not counting bones. How much meat do you figure that trailer carries? Ten tons tops."

"What do you suggest we do?"

"First off, all the seeds in town should be gathered up and planted in fertile open spaces so the people will have vegetables to eat, even flowers if need be. Next, search parties should be set up to scour the woods for berries and edible wild mushrooms. The berries can be eaten now or made into preserves.

"When this town was first founded ninety years ago, I'm sure people did such things to supplement what they bought. With the coming of civilization and supermarkets people forgot the basics. Well, now they're going to have to learn them again. And that's not all. You'll have to organize hunting parties to start bringing in wild deer, elk, ducks, geese, and other animal life. Also fishing parties to supplement the meat diet. I've got plenty of hunting experience and will help out there. But I'm sure I'm not the only man here who can do that.''

"There are plenty," Willem answered. "But I'm thinking further down the line. A few million people can live off the woods. But a lot more may have survived. I'm sure tens of millions died in the bombings. However, tens of millions more are still alive. This country can't feed them all off the products of the wild. Eventually, we'll over-fish and over-hunt and then there'll be nothing left."

"True," Stack answered. "But right now we have to look at what's going down in the next few weeks. Let's take this one step at a time. Later, we can look farther down the road. At present there are more critical problems. The local power plant wasn't touched and there's coal for a month. Water and gas are still flowing. But how long will these items last? We were far enough out of the way not to get hit. But gas lines get supplied from farther afield and that flow's surely been interrupted somewhere down the line, which means the shortage will come here. Water will last till the local pumps run out of fuel or break. People will have to go back to digging wells, getting water from streams in the woods, cooking and heating with wood, living without electricity, going to the bathroom in outhouses. I don't think they realize how primitive life will get. It may look romantic in all those cowboy movies, but the reality of those times was hard and harsh. Things are always romantic when viewed from long ago and far away, but Little House On The Prairie was a rough thing to experience firsthand."

Willem grinned. "It's a lot better than the alternative— being dead."

"I can't disagree with that, but we've got to prepare now."

"Fine. Let me think on it till tonight. As for now, why don't you go see your girl?"

"Sure." The smile on Stack's face fled to be replaced by

a grim look as Willem drove him to the Winston house.

When they arrived, he got out of the car, bid Willem
goodbye, then headed up the walk to the front door as the
sheriff drove off, Stack knocked once and the door came
open as if they had been waiting for him, not even allowing
him time to gather his thoughts.

"She's awake," Mrs. Winston said, a worried look on
her face as she welcomed him in. Nancy, her daughter and
Rayisa's friend, came into the room and smiled weakly at
Stack.

"Everything okay now?" Mrs. Winston asked.

"As okay as such things ever are," he answered,
thinking about the dead to be buried, the wounded to be
healed, the psychic wounds which would last for decades.

Meanwhile, Mrs. Winston led him to Rayisa's room. He
wondered if they'd have to call the town physician, Doctor
Ozeron, to give Rayisa another sedative so she could bear
the coming day. But he forgot about that as he reached her
door and knocked. For one second there was no reply,
then, from within, a weak, almost hesitant voice asked,
"Who is it, Nancy?"

"It's me, Rayisa."

"Oh, Nick," she gasped, a sudden catch to her voice,
which sounded relieved to hear him. Nick Stack, man of
the hour and security blanket. She ran from the bed, her
nightgown fluttering around her bare ankles, as he opened
the door and stepped into the room. Rayisa ran to him,
grasped him around the waist, put her face against his
chest, and sobbed out her anguish. Stack, still numb from
lack of sleep and the horrors of the combat he had undergone, put his arms around her, rubbed her head, and tried
to be as supportive as possible. Still, the words would not
come. The jumble of thoughts in his head would not clear.
The things he'd planned to say did not leave his lips. Stack
silently damned himself, but remained tongue-tied, and
did the only thing he could, squeezing Rayisa tightly to him
as his body trembled with the sobs which wracked her
small, frail form.

He felt the wetness of her tears soak through his shirt and was aware of the grime of the night, feeling somehow filthy that he had come to her this way without showering first. But in the end it did not matter.

Finally, her sobbing abated. She pulled back a little, his arms falling from her in response. Rayisa looked up at Stack, her eyes red, her nose running, her face glistening with tears, and asked, "Why weren't you here when I woke up, like you promised?"

The question, full of the innocence of a child, cut him, but he held back, not realizing he could be so emotional till then. Perhaps this was only temporary, the result of the shock of war and the things he had done. It made Stack aware that much molding was still needed to make him the man of steel he was supposed to be and looked like from outside.

"The battling was harder and longer than expected," he answered. "But I still came as fast as possible. The drive from Vista Royale is nearly forty miles."

"Yes, I see." She went and sat on her mussed bed. On a side table was a half-finished breakfast. He went and sat down beside her, indenting the bed as he put an arm around Rayisa, who looked down at her toes.

"Is there anything you want to talk about?"

"No," Rayisa said unconvincingly. He didn't push her to talk. Nor did he give her any pop psychology about how good it would feel to bring it all out. Maybe it would just make it worse. He often felt worse when he talked out his insides. But there was no time to dwell on what might be. Rayisa began to talk. And, as she did, Stack reflected on how events moved him along more than he moved them. He felt more and more like a cork bobbing on an endless, alien sea. But he said nothing as she spoke about what had been going on inside of her.

"That kidnapping was the hardest thing that ever happened to me, Nick. Harder than seeing what became of Fresno and finding out that my parents were no longer alive." She looked him straight in the eyes.

"I was surprised you didn't cry then."

"Maybe I was too stunned. But I'm crying now, Nick."
He saw the tears that had started down her cheeks again
and reflected on how mature she'd suddenly become.

Then Rayisa stopped crying and said, "When they kidnapped me, I went numb, I was like that till they forced me
to undress at knifepoint. Then they began beating me with
that belt, telling me what they wanted me to do. I didn't
ever think I could get down on my knees like that and take
that man's thing in my mouth." She cringed, but continued. "And then you arrived and saved me. It all
happened so fast. There was gunfire and then people were
dying around me. But after what they did none of it
bothered me."

He put an arm around her, gave Rayisa a squeeze, and
said, "That's the way you're supposed to feel. Those men
were renegades, bandits, murderers. They did horrible
things and deserved what they got. Don't regret how you
feel. You should have cheered what happened. And one
day you may. But the thing now is for you to allow yourself to heal and get over this horror."

"Oh, Nick." She began to sob and threw herself against
his chest. He put his arms around her. "I don't think I'll
ever recover. I can't forget this. It was so terrible, so very
terrible."

"Yes, yes, I know. But the valleys are always darkest till
we head up into the sunlit mountains where we're
supposed to live. Do you understand that? I don't mean
mountains like we're in now, but the mountains that
represent the highs in our heads."

"I understand," she mumbled in a muffled voice because her face was buried against his chest. Then she pulled
back, wiped her eyes, and sat staring forward.

"You didn't finish your breakfast," he said, pointing to
it.

"I'm not very hungry."

"I wouldn't be either. But you've got to keep up your
strength. Things are going to get so much harder than
they've been so far."

She looked at him with sudden concern. "You mean more bikers will be coming?"

"No. But the food supply, water, gas, and a hundred other things we depend on to make up our civilization will quickly disappear in the form we've known them. And there will be more radiation sickness and perhaps some deaths. So you've got to eat to be strong. Force yourself."

She nodded, took a piece of toast off the plate, and began to absentmindedly munch on it. He watched her eat a moment, then rose and said, "Let me go so I don't disturb your breakfast."

She stopped chewing. "You're leaving?"

"Only for the moment. After breakfast, when you've bathed and dressed, we can go for a walk outside town, if you want, and talk about anything that's on your mind."

"All right," she said with a feeble smile.

Stack nodded and left, stopping to tell Mrs. Winston and Nancy that Rayisa was a little better and still eating breakfast. Then he left the house, drained by the experience, realizing his energy reserves had been sapped but that this was only the beginning of a long journey.

Stack took the last cigarette from his pack before throwing it away. He then lit the cigarette and inhaled, but hardly felt the smoke going down as his mind focused on other things. He was worried about Rayisa because he had to leave this place soon. What would he do about the girl? He couldn't just leave her. He was her security blanket. Yet at the same time he had an even greater responsibility to his family. Stack gnashed his teeth as he wrestled with this double dilemma, trying at the same time to deal with the hourly stimuli bombarding him; the questions, the threats, and the obsatcles he faced at every twist and turn.

How he missed the recent past. Stack smiled briefly as his mind shifted back several days to the woods where he had been camping without a care or worry in the world; fishing, exploring, and hunting. The world had been his oyster and he had been one of the pearls. And then this. To fall from the heights into the depths. He wouldn't even

have been in California if not for an aunt who'd died and
left money, stocks, bonds, and property to Nick and his
relatives. Nick had been chosen to go West and dispose of
the inheritance. He'd wired the money to a bank back
East, mailed the stocks and bonds to New York, and sold
the property. Following all this, he'd figured he owed
himself four days' vacation, had taken it in the woods near
here.

But a sudden nuclear war has broken out after a
simmering crisis over Persian Gulf oil, civil war in Iran,
Russian troop deployments in that country, and a war
between Syria and Israel. The war between Syria and Israel
was one Russia had helped stir up. Syria had lost after two
weeks of savage fighting that had left them with 10,000
military dead and 1300 tanks and tank-type vehicles such
as mobile-missile platforms and self-propelled artillery
destroyed and captured by Israel. Russia had quickly
stepped in to get an armistice, and had begun resupplying
the stunned and bloodied Syrians. But by that time
American and Soviet ships, NATO and Soviet fleets were
clashing at sea. Castro was making ominous noises in
Havana. And the entire thing had bubbled over just as it
looked as if everything was about to be settled. Someone,
somewhere, had miscalculated. The missiles had begun to
fly and the bombs had started to fall. Stack didn't know
who pushed the buttons first, though he strongly suspected
it was the Russians. Nor did he know what straw had
broken the camel's back. But the end result, which lay
before his eyes, was that tens of millions of survivors
found themselves in a quandary without end. And the
worst horrors, he suspected, were yet to come.

By the time he had finished thinking this through he had
reached Willem's office on Main Street. Willem was there,
at his desk, doing some quick paperwork. Messengers were
coming in and out. Telephone service, except for radios
and walkie-talkies, was gone.

Willem looked up as Stalk walked into the small,
cluttered, one-man office. "Sit down," he said, pointing

to a chair in the left corner of the room. It was full of the memorabilia of the professional lawman, from pictures to plaques to scrolls on the walls, as well as the guns, communications gear, filing cabinets, and papers strewn here, there, and everywhere.

Stack sat down, leaned back, crossed his legs, and watched Willem, who said, "I'll be with you as soon as I finish tallying the supplies in town. I've asked every household to let me know what they have because we may soon start rationing, with those who have more giving to those who have less."

Willem picked up a cigarette from a green glass ashtray near his elbow, took a quick pull on the butt, expelled smoke, and began talking through the bluish-gray cloud rising around his head.

"In a day or two we'll begin sending out hunting and fishing parties and start planting all the seeds we have. That'll keep us going for awhile."

"Sounds good," Stack said. "But do you think people will really help each other and share?"

Willem looked him straight in the eyes. "Sure they will. This is small-town America, not big-city New York. People aren't as self-centered."

"Everyone's self-centered when their ass is on the line. It's me or the other guy, so the other guy's going to eat the bullet. That's how people think when you get down to brass tacks. They're all the same."

"I beg to differ. You're big-city. You see with big-city eyes. You've never lived in a small town all your life. I have."

A messenger walked in. A high school kid with a sheaf of papers. He handed them to Willem, looked inquiringly at Stack, then left. Stack now replied.

"I may be big-city, but I'm not blind to human nature and I'm nobody's fool. I come from a family that always liked to hunt, camp, fish, hike, and canoe. We've been all over and have experienced many different types of towns and country environments. Sure, the people there are different from big-city folks. They may even be nicer. But in the end people are pretty much the same when faced with their own demise.''

"I don't think so," Willem said, taking another drag on his cigarette. "I think you'll agree when you see how they perform under stress. When the chips are down these are some of the sweetest people you'll find on the planet earth outside the pearly gates of Eden."

"You sound like a travelogue for the mountains. Come on up, folks, and we'll give you good, home-grown food, and clear spring water. Of course, the water's slightly polluted by radiation and so's the food. But don't worry. All it'll give you is periodic diarrhea and you'll glow at night. That way your friends will be able to find you in the dark and you won't need a light when going to the bathroom at three in the morning."

Willem grinned. "At least you haven't lost your sense of humor."

"I didn't realize I had one till this bastard war came around. As for losing my sense of humor, it's nothing to worry about. What should worry you is when this town loses its sense of humor, if anything is left of it by now. And when the water stops running and they can't turn on the gas because there isn't any, tempers will run hot."

"I know that, but we have streams all around and plenty of firewood." Willem gestured toward the woods surrounding Montieth. His window looked out on the alley next to the store across the way.

"What about locations which don't have great stands of woods?"

"They'll forage in the rubble of houses for it, or use bushes, dried grass, and such till the oil and gas lines can be repaired and start pumping again."

Stack's laugh was more like a short bark. "You're dreaming, Kurt. The producing fields have probably been destroyed by nuclear strikes. It will take years to put out the well fires and new wells will have to be drilled. There may be no shortage of oil or gas in the ground, but you have to get it out to the consumer, and this country is in damn bad shape. Here in the mountains you won't see that, but go down to Fresno, like I did. Then you'll see the hell. And I'm sure there are dozens, if not hundreds, of cities like it."

"Yeah, but this country can regenerate itself."

"Sounds good in theory. I just don't think it'll work in practice."

"We'll see. Time will tell who's right."

"If we live that long. Some big nightmares are looming on the horizon. Don't forget that for one moment. This is only the third day of the war. It's no time to be getting cocky about what will happen in the future. Forget oil and gas. Those are products of intact high-technology societies. The attack we've undergone and the attacks we may yet undergo have pushed us back, in many cases, into the last century—as so many will find out. The only high-tech fuel we can depend on is old-fashioned coal. And it'll be produced the old way by small bands in primitive, dangerous mining operations, the way it used to be done decades ago. And the big factories which survived this war won't be working either. Man may have been climbing for the stars before this hell began, but he sure is down in the mud now. Falling down a mountain is a hell of a lot easier than climbing up." Stack stopped, smiled sheepishly, and said, "Sorry for sounding like a speech, but I had to lay out the record as I see it."

"I appreciate that, Nick, and will take it into consideration."

"There's more," Stack said as he rose from the chair. "I can't stay here. I've got to get back East to my family. This," he pointed to the ground, "is your world. But mine's back there. I have a family to find. Who knows what happened to them," he said, his face suddenly grim. "And I wonder what they think happened to me. In the end that may be the worst part of wars and disasters. You don't know if there were survivors and the tension of waiting and not knowing is almost as bad as seeing the dead bodies of loved ones."

Willem listened in silence, thinking of the brother he had lost. "You have folks?" Stack suddenly asked. "I may be prying, but I know so little about you though we've been through some hard stuff together."

"There isn't much to tell. My parents are both dead. Dad went first, then Mom, two years later. Dad was killed when his car went off the road in icy weather about fifty miles from here near an abandoned gold mine known as the Parker Lode. Mom passed away due to natural causes. Wyatt, whom you already know about, died trying to defend Vista Royale. My other brother, Quentin, succumbed to liver cancer three years ago. And my two sisters, both of whom live in other states, may or may not be dead." He shrugged. "That's my family history. A thumbnail sketch. You'd think so many lives covering decades and decades would have more to them."

"They probably do," Stack said, "but you need a good writer to go in there and mine out the nuggets worth preserving and weave them into a family saga."

Willem smiled briefly. "You mean like one of those six-part paperback sagas women love to read so much?" Stack nodded. "I'll keep that in mind," he added as he got back to business.

"I understand about your family," Willem added. "But how will you get back? You're no eagle. You haven't got wings."

"But the crew of the bomber we rescued does. They can take me far enough east for me to find other transport back the rest of the way."

"You're dreamin' mister. You're talkin' about three thousand miles of terrain, not thirty. What about your van? Are you willing it to me? And why not just make the trip in your van?"

Stack blew out a gust of air. "I didn't even think about it. But if I can get a plane east I'll just leave it here. I know the van has value, but there are things one must place above the value of mere material objects, if you get my drift.'' Willem nodded. ''Besides, taking a van cross-country creates problems. I might not be able to get enough fuel, or if something breaks, I might find myself stranded in the middle of nowhere with no guarantee of getting repairs, or finding someone with the right parts. And a plane can get me back East fast, which is what I want.''

''You're betting on some pretty big ifs, son. The plane didn't land at that deserted airfield for the crew's health. Some mighty big things are wrong with it.''

''Perhaps they'll still try to take it up. I want to be aboard when they do.''

''You're assuming they'll go East. What if they try for Siberia?''

''That's why I want to talk to them.''

''I'll take you there. But what about the girl? Rayisa will need you more now than ever.''

Stack frowned. ''I know. But I can't stay.''

''You're going to abandon her?'' Willem asked, his face suddenly hard.

''I don't know what to do,'' Stack said throwing his hands out, then letting them fall into his lap. Finally, he rose. ''Let me go see her again. I'll figure out what to do.''

''I'll wait for you. I still have work to do.''

''Fine,'' Stack said, and hurried back to the Winston home. Mrs. Winston was standing in her open doorway nervously smoking a cigarette and talking to a neighboring housewife when Stack came up the walk. Both women turned to him.

''Rayisa all finished with breakfast?'' he asked.

''I guess so,'' Mrs. Winston replied. ''She'll be glad to see you back.''

He nodded to both women as he self-consciously entered the house, aware of their eyes boring into him as he headed toward Rayisa's room. As he entered it, she jumped up from the bed and ran to him. They embraced, but she let go of him right away and stepped back to look at Stack.

''Come, let's sit down,'' he said. They went and sat on

the bed. As they did, he looked at the breakfast tray. Most of the food had been eaten. "Good," he said with a smile.

Stack wanted to hesitate, but knew if he did the words he wanted to say would stick in his throat and this bull had to be seized by the horns now.

"Rayisa," he began, hoping his voice sounded soft, kind, and concerned. "Perhaps, now that you've gone through all this, you'd like me to take you back to your aunt in Makepiece. I'm sure she's worried about you and will be glad to know you're safe. Also, it'll feel secure for you to be there."

Rayisa shook her head. "Not while I'm like this. I want to get better first. Then I might go back. Mrs. Winston says I can stay here as long as I want. And I have Nancy, my good friend, here."

"All right, if that's what you want. But your aunt loves you too and she'll also be good for you."

"Maybe later," Rayisa said with a tone of finality. Stack now saw he had to broach the truth and tell her about his family and objectives. He hesitated, but before inaction could grasp him by the throat, he began.

"You know, Rayisa, I have a family. A girl about your age, two sons, a wife. . . ." She had been staring at the wall, but now looked at him.

"I know. You told me about them when I was thumbing a ride to Fresno and you picked me up."

"I miss them very much," he plowed on, not wanting to look at her, but forcing himself to do so. "I don't know if they're alive or dead and they don't know what's happened to me. I owe them and they owe me. And for those reasons I have to find them." He fell silent as her eyes, tears in them now, burned through him.

"But you promised you'd stay. You promised you'd be there whenever I needed you. . . ." Her voice died away.

"I was in pain because of your pain," he answered, the pain now evident in his voice and face. "So I said things I meant without thinking of other obligations."

"That's why you want me to go to my aunt?" she said accusingly.

"That's one of the reasons."

"But you're going to desert me now and forget all about me."

"No," he said with finality. "If you need me and don't want to go to your aunt, I'll take you with me. I meant it when I said I'd be there when you needed me."

Rayisa began to sob and threw herself against his chest. "You're my only family now. I'll follow you anywhere." She pulled back and looked up at him through tear-filled eyes. "When will I be leaving with you?"

"I'm going to see some people soon, then I'll return here and we'll know where we stand." Stack kissed Rayisa, bade her goodbye, and quickly left.

Willem was waiting out front when Stack returned to the sheriff's office. They got into the police cruiser and drove off. Willem looked at Stack and said, "I've been talking to someone in town who knows an old moonshiner who lives up in the hills and owns a still he occasionally fires up. We can get him to make some changes in his operation and begin producing wood alcohol. It can be used in engines adjusted for the process. The conversion operation isn't difficult. And that'll give us the fuel we need when regular supplies run out, which shouldn't be long."

"So you'll be making gasahol?"

"No. There won't be enough fuel for that. We'll be burning pure alcohol. People may even begin making coal-run, steam-engine-powered vehicles the way the Germans did toward the end of World War II. They had a hell of a lot of coal and not enough fuel. We, on the other hand, have the fuel, but can't get it out of the ground and refined. At least for now. Of course, we may be jumping to conclusions. Things may not be so bad as we believe."

"Now it's my turn to say you're dreaming. Most disasters, personal as well as national, are often worse than people imagine them to be."

"You really know how to cheer a guy up," Willem said sarcastically.

"I just didn't want you raising your hopes too high, then having them dashed."

"Makes sense," Willem said as he reached for another cigarette from the half-empty pack on his dashboard.

"What'll you do when the butts run out?" Stack asked with a smile.

"I'll grow my own tobacco, the way settlers did in the old days. I'll cure the leaves, then smoke them in the form of cigars, or in a corncob pipe."

"Sounds romantic."

"I'm sure when we've lived awhile that way we'll wax nostalgic about the good old days before the war."

Stack grinned. "What happens if the world repairs itself and we return to the way things were? Will we look back at the way things are now and say we didn't realize how good we had it?"

"Possibly. People are funny that way." Stack nodded without saying anything and both men dropped off into a long silence, each anchored deeply in their own thoughts.

Willem, turning off the main road, shifted him from his thoughts. Stack saw that they were moving along a dusty trail that would take them by twists and turns down to the bottom of the five-mile-long, one-mile-wide valley where the landing strip and the B-52 were located.

They came over a rise and before them stretched the valley, bordered on all sides by 8000- and 9000-foot peaks, each blanketed with an undulating blue-green carpet of hundreds of thousands of trees, mostly pines and spruces. Sharp, angry granite peaks loomed out of the greenery like talons ripping at the blue of the sky and the lower clouds, which teased the peaks with fat, soft, thick bellies full of moisture that on occasion rained down across the mountains and woods. Only now these serene and pure-looking clouds were full of radiation-laden water and any rain which fell would damage the men, animals, and vegetation in its path.

These things were only dimly on the minds of the two

men as Willem carefully maneuvered his vehicle over ruts, dips, and rises, trying to avoid potholes, fallen trees, and rock slides which partly blocked the way.

Down at the bottom of the valley there were few trees amid the mostly undulating grassland marked by a 9000-foot runway which, except for the last 200 feet, where rusted metal ribs showed through the concrete, had been completed before the project had been abandoned for lack of money. This had once been the proposed airfield for a retirement community vacation center with hotels and a shopping center. But it was too far into the wilderness and the landing and takeoff pattern required was too dangerous for less experienced pilots who had to come suddenly up over the mountains, then dip down into the valley to reach the runway, and on taking off climb sharply for height to avoid the talon peaks of the mountain rims waiting to rip out their guts. For a pilot having to use this airfield in bad weather, it would be ulcer city.

The police cruiser now started down into the valley. Its floor was 4500 feet above sea level. In the far distance was the camouflaged brown, yellow, and green B-52. He was surprised at how big it looked, even at this distance. He was also surprised at how hazardous the descent into the valley was by car—something he had not realized when they made the trip in darkness. It had also been more dangerous then.

Finally, after a jolting ride, they reached the bottom and began to make their way across the grass to the landing strip. A highway had been planned through the mountains into this valley. But only a rough access road had been built so that raw materials, construction equipment, and work crews could be brought in. Since the project had been abandoned, the road had become mostly overgrown. The B-52 would have picked a better place to come down had one been available. The crew had flown over most of southern California, looking down on cratered, bombed-out, debris-covered airfields, military and civilian.

The cruiser made swift progress across the grassy valley

despite the fact that the two passengers were thrown about
by the ride as the car dipped up and down and rocked from
side to side, sending up a light brown dust cloud which
snaked out behind them, coating the windows and filling
the inside of the car with a stifling cloud, some of which
the men swallowed before rolling up the windows. And
then it was over as they touched concrete and began racing
along the runway, the distance between them and the plane
rapidly shrinking as the bomber grew in size till it looked
like some giant out of Atlantis. Willem began applying the
brakes and honked a few times in case those guarding the
plane mistook them for possible attackers. But the men
around the aircraft raised their sidearms in a wave and
knew they were friends. A clearly marked sheriff's car
wouldn't be mistaken for an enemy unless the guards
thought hooligans had stolen it.

The car finally came to a stop 50 feet short of the
bomber. Stack looked up in awe at how huge it was.
Nearly five stories from the wheels on the tarmac to the top
of the tail, 160 feet from nose to rear, 180 feet from
wingtip to wingtip, nearly 250 tons of plane able to travel
7500 miles without refueling on 46,000 gallons of fuel.
Enough to heat two dozen private homes for one year.

There was no more time to marvel at this immense
creation which had perhaps been brought down by a defect
in a ten-cent part. The two men got out of the police
cruiser, shutting their doors simultaneously. The bomber
crew and some of the members of the Harley-Davidson
motorcycle club that had been passing through Montieth
and helped drive the hooligan bikers out of Vista Royale
while protecting the bomber came forward. The B-52
crew—Commander Giles Garudet, Copilot Brad Osseville,
Navigator Bob Carbindell, and ECM warfare man Lance
Briggs—came toward them first, followed by the leader of
the Harley-Davidson club, Bay Courtner, and some of his
men. Of the other two members of the bomber crew, one
had been killed and the other had been wounded.

"How's everything?" Garudet asked as he shook

Willem's hand, then Stack's. Courtner came over and they also shook hands. Stack then quickly got down to the reason for his coming and told them about his family in New York. He asked if they might possibly be heading in that direction, or, if not, how far east they could take him. He had to find his family and see how they were.

Garudet listened, looked at Osseville, and finally said, "You're out of luck." He looked at the plane for a second. "There's too much wrong to chance taking this bird up, which is why we came down in the middle of nowhere. If some mechanics could look the bomber over and repair the problem, there'd be no sweat taking you someplace closer to home, if not all the way East. But there's been a helluva war, in case nobody's noticed. And there aren't any repair facilities waiting for us, and no mechanics who can repair this kind of plane at your local friendly airbases, most of which no longer exist. So we'll have to wait till we find an airfield. We started the engines earlier in order to use the communications gear to try and contact some Air Force HQ, near or far. We tried every possible frequency and got zilch. That's where it stands."

"But there must be some intact fields still around," Stack said.

"Sure. Only we can't get through. The electromagnetic pulses sent out by the exploding bombs lobotomized many sending and receiving units. However, if you're willing to get word to some military authority that there's a jet here in need of repairs, full of bombs, and available to fly on to Siberia or anywhere else, we'll be glad, once out of here, to take you nearer to your home, maybe even to New York. I can't guarantee that, you understand."

"Mister, you've got yourself a deal. I spoke to a Major Bill Bathhurst a few days ago in Fresno. He was part of a surviving National Guard unit sent down from the San Francisco HQ to save lives and bring out the injured, though not too many survivors were around to be rescued."

"I didn't expect there to be," Garudet said. "Not after

what hit them. But if you can get to the San Francisco HQ, where the real authority lies, you might be able to get this information passed up the chain of command to where it would eventually get back to some Air Force unit, which could pass on instructions for you to bring to us and maybe even get some mechanics here. Would there be any problem for you to go to Frisco?''

'None at all.'' At this point Courtner broke in.

"If you're going to San Francisco, our Harley-Davidson club can join you and help find the military people in command. We planned to go down there anyway to search for the relatives of one of our members who live in Sausalito, across from San Francisco. I already explained to you last night that we're part of a Harley-Davidson user club which travels the country attending various events. The war caught us in the mountains, and now we have to find out the whereabouts of our loved ones. Since we're a team, each of us is going to travel to the homes of the other members to help him find his relatives.''

"Good to have you along,'' Stack said. Then he turned to Willem. "Wanna come, Kurt?''

"Unfortunately, I have rationing to organize, hunting parties to set up. Talking about food, I hope you guys watching this bomber here have enough to eat and drink. If not, let me know and I'll send someone along with victuals.''

Then he looked at Stack. "I'll also have to get me a deputy and take over the function of law in Vista Royale now that Wyatt's gone.'' His voice caught for a second. He looked around and said, "Losing a brother ain't easy. I know that sounds small after a war like this when so many paid the ultimate price. But it still hurts. A brother ain't like losing any old thing. When two men have a lifetime of dreams, hopes, and secrets together, and then one of them leaves this life before his time, especially the way he went, it hurts. Still, a man must carry on with the things of today so he can survive tomorrow and the days which will surely follow it. Yet you can't help but remember the way times were, and are no more, while doing the other things.''

Then Willem fell silent. Maybe baring his soul wasn't his style. Or perhaps he just felt naked in that moment and stopped. It didn't matter. They understood. Each had suffered, and respected him more for having said what he did.

"Well," he finally said, "I guess talking won't do much for the living, or the dead." Then, looking at Courtner and Stack, he added, "Why don't you get on with what it is you have to do. I'll get you fuel, if you need it, and water and food too." With that, he headed back to the police cruiser and Stack hurried after him.

2

Nick Stack, in his red and black van, a cigarette between his lips, led the Harley-Davidson motorcycle convoy down from the mountains. Most of the bikers followed along behind him, but some overtook him, riding alongside or moving out ahead, the drivers smiling back almost as if this was some jaunt in the country, not a mission into hell to find possible survivors and pass on information about a bomber which might and might not get him back to his family. So much uncertainty, so many obstacles, so many unanswered questions. The great stone on his shoulders had turned into a boulder, and pressed down so hard that his thoughts had become as real as the pines, spruces, bushes, and fields which flew by on both sides of the road, the trees sometimes forming an overhead canopy that sent dappled shadows flying across his face and the swiftly moving van.

Stack watched the cavorting riders and grinned a grin of death. Didn't they know millions were now dead? Of course they knew. But the human spirit was irrepressible and kept smiling inside despite the tears and bile and blackness and gall. The face which did not look up at the sun and bask in its reflections was the face of a soul already dead. He realized his now more so than at any time in his life and looked at himself in the mirror, wondering if perhaps he was already a dead man. Stack could not rejoice. He could only mourn and worry and wonder.

He looked at the sky. It was bright, though not as bright as before the war, because of some overcast. Was this due to the radioactive dust in the atmosphere, the beginning of a nuclear winter? He didn't know, and the uncertainty only made the expression on his face grimmer still.

"Damnit, smile. Shine out like those others," he thought to himself. But he couldn't. It was not his style and never would be. A man could not be other than himself, following the pattern of his insides in all his ways with the world.

They came down from the mountains in stages, noticing distant glints of metal from moving vehicles. Far off, three blackish-brown pillars of smoke indicated fierce fires along the coast. An aftermath of the blasts. Stack scanned the sky, but saw no aircraft or helicopters.

By the time they were down to 3000 feet in elevation there were more fields, some farms with cattle in the meadows but no farmers in sight, and then the first town, untouched by nuclear blasts, with people in the streets. Stack stopped the van and the motorcyclists stopped behind and around him. An older man in his 60s came over. They talked quickly, both of their faces grim.

"Where you from?" the man asked as a small, silent, sullen crowd gathered.

"Montieth. How're things here?"

"Not bad, could be worse."

"You have electricity, running water, gas?"

The man grinned briefly. "Nothing. It stopped the first day of the war. You have these things in Montieth?"

"Yeah."

"Lucky."

"Any casualties here?"

"Half the kids in town went off by bus for a field trip to Frisco only hours before the war began. None's come back. We've sent people out looking for them. None have yet returned. The parents, needless to say, are distraught as hell."

"How many kids?"

"Fifty-seven."

"What a bitch. How're things otherwise? Is there enough food? How's the radiation problem?"

"Food's running low, but we sent a group of men to an abandoned farm nearby. The farmer's run off and they're killing the cattle and chickens for meat. So there's no worry there. Another farm, where the owner stayed, has been selling us vegetables at prices which aren't too inflated. Naturally, no one can vouch for the levels of radiation in the food. But people got to eat, right?" Stack added.

Then the old man said, "The radiation's hit us hard in some cases, light in other cases. Two old sisters up and died. They were sickly anyhow and this just pushed them over the edge. We also lost a baby, two months old. How about in Montieth?"

"Nobody yet. But it's still early in the war. There'll be more."

"I'm sure of it." The old man looked at the bikers and asked Stack, "Where are you people headin' for?"

"The Bay Area. One of our people has relatives that he wants to find."

"I wish you luck. The Bay Area's been hit damn bad."

"Have any idea why the war began? All I know is bits and pieces."

"Can't tell you nuthin'. Radio's dead. No TV. No papers."

"Can you sell us any gasoline?"

"We need all our fuel. But I'll ask around. Wait." The man disappeared through the crowd. Stack lit a cigarette and drummed a thumb on the steering wheel. The man returned in a few minutes.

"Sorry," he said. "Nobody wants to sell."

"I understand. Thanks for trying. I've got to be moving on. Nice seeing you. Maybe we'll meet again on our way back."

"Sure thing," the man said, waving feebly as Stack

started off and the crowd parted for him and the bikers. The convoy quickly left the town behind, moving once more through green country that was blackened in places where reflected heat from the nuclear blasts had started fires which had been put out, or, more likely, died away in the rains that followed the attack. The rains that had fallen after the nuclear blasts, except in the desert, had washed away the grime of radiation, but also brought it to other places.

They went past farms, these with farmers in the fields talking to each other over fences. The men in the convoy did not have to stop and buy anything. They had enough provisions. However, on the way back they might need to. But their combined dollar resources were not large, and they would probably not be able to buy much at the high prices they would be charged.

Another town loomed up. This one was closer to the coast. Roofs, partly or totally, had been ripped off most houses. Windows were gone. Small sheds had been knocked down, some cars had been set on fire. There were many people in the streets, most not injured, and light traffic moving in all directions.

"How're things along the coast?" Stack called out to a passing truck.

"Don't know," the man behind the wheel called back. "Didn't come from there." And then he was gone.

Stack saw a sheriff's deputy, slowed down, called out to him, and asked how things were around the Bay Area.

"Forget it," the freckle-faced kid, no more than 19, called back. "Don't even go there. Almost total devastation. Hundreds of thousands dead."

Stack nodded and drove on. They were soon out of town and moving along country roads again. There were houses here and there and some roadside stores, two of them, amazingly, still open. Abandoned cars lined the road. Stack honked and began to pull off the road; the bikers followed him.

He got out of the van as the others got off their bikes

and formed a half circle around him. "This may be a long trip," Stack said. "We'll need fuel. Little is for sale and that may be priced at five or ten dollars a gallon. Prices simply unacceptable on our budget."

"That's a fact," one of the bikers, Joe Angelicus, said. He was tall, tanned, with short, silky black hair on a long, lean head. His piercing brown eyes watched like a hawk and didn't miss a detail.

"These abandoned vehicles are most probably full of fuel. Some may have been abandoned because they were out of gas, others due to mechanical reasons or because the owners came down with the effects of radiation poisoning or deep wounds. What we've got to do now is transfer their fuel into our gas tanks."

He held up a length of narrow, yellowed, clear plastic hose given him by a man up in Montieth before Stack had gone down to Fresno. He showed it to Courtner, whose small mouth opened in wonder as he scratched his spade jaw.

"Stick one end in the gas tank you want to empty, the other end in your mouth, then make believe you're drinking Bosco through a straw. When the gasoline moves two-thirds of the way up the tube, hold your breath, pull the hose out, shove it into your gas tank and take your mouth away. Keep repeating it till your tank is full. Do not go past the two-thirds mark on the tube. It may mean more trips between gas tanks, but less chance of swallowing any gasoline, which is a poison. You'll either get very sick or die. Only rudimentary health facilities are available, and none can be easily found."

He then asked who wanted to go first, and one of the bikers raised his hand. While he began transferring fuel, the others waited. No one smoked. It took them, with each man waiting his turn, about two hours to complete the process. Then the journey began again. They took a detour to cut several miles off the trip and found themselves moving along a road blasted out of the side of a mountain, with tall, weathered granite walls on one flank and a sharp

300-foot drop into a long, narrow valley on their right.

They moved along at 40 miles an hour, eyes alert, ready to slow down and stop on this narrow roadway in case traffic appeared around a curve ahead going in the opposite direction.

Some of the bikers had moved out ahead of the van. Suddenly, one of the lead bikers began to slow down, gesticulating wildly with his left arm. The riders up front barely stopped in time, and Stack after them. A quick glance in the rearview mirror showed that the bikers behind had also come to a dead halt. What had stopped the convoy was just ahead and coming straight at them.

A great, gray carpet of tens of thousands of rats. Fat, furry bodies, flailing tails like an endless sea of snakes standing up from the earth, as they moved down the rock face from higher up, then across the road and down into the valley below. The sound of their crossing was like thousands of magnified tiny clicks as the nails on their feet struck the asphalt. This mixed with the high keening voices of the mega herd, which created a deafening babel. The cloud of dust raised by their passing added a brownish hue to the undulating gray mass.

The horror of all this for Stack was leavened by the knowledge that rat and lice invasions occurred after disasters, especially nuclear blasts, as in Hiroshima and Nagasaki. The vermin sensed the dead meat. It was feast time. And so they were racing down from every hole they occupied toward the coastal cities. Perhaps they had gotten the message late, or had traveled several days to get to this point, their mass growing larger, deadlier, more hellish by the hour.

The motorcyclists in front began to turn around, and headed back down the road in the narrow space between the van and the rock wall. The rats were also turning. They had scented the living meat. And there were so many of them now that they were the hunters and did not fear man anymore.

A film of sweat broke out across Stack's face as he

began to turn the van around, the bikers having fled several hundred yards down the road to watch what was happening up ahead. Frantically, he realized there wasn't enough width on the road to make a fast U-turn. He had to make a broken U-turn, stopping to swing the van this way and that. And all of it cost him precious seconds during which the carpet of rats raced forward until the great gray front engulfed the van.

Stack hissed as the huge herd ran between and around the wheels, moving out in front of the van while others climbed up the sides, their nails clicking across the roof and windows. Rat climbing over rat. Rat holding onto rat until the deadly gray carpet quickly covered every square inch and Stack had to stop, unable to complete the U-turn because he was unable to see out and afraid he would go off the cliff and end his life in a fiery crash down below. And then the rats would have achieved their purpose as surely as if they had gnawed every bit of living flesh off his body, even if he took thousands of them with him.

As he sat there, trapped and watching, rats swarmed over the van, looking for a way in. Yellowed fangs, gnashing teeth, open, pink-tongued mouths, bristly whiskers, red, beedy eyes—all were on him, all were ready to bite into his flesh, moving this way and that, sniffing for a way in. Stack could almost smell their hot, fetid, hungry breath and it made his skin crawl, filling him with the alien horror most men have felt for rats from time immemorial. He had to get out of there!

Stack kept his cool and tried to estimate his position on the road before the rats had overrun the van, and then he began to drive slowly forward, feeling his way, the van shaking with the movement, some of the gray creatures falling off to be squashed under the tires, leaving behind bloody, furry muck. And then he tried to straighten out and move along ever so slowly in case he was near the edge. If that were so, Stack would feel it as one tire began to rotate over open air. This did not happen. Instead, more rats fell off. In a few places he saw through the mass, recognized his position on the road, and took on added speed. Animals continued to drop off, being crunched flat under the wheels. The van moved faster, looking like a big bundle of fur, as squeals of fright were torn from rats now clinging to the outside of the vehicle for dear life as more of them were shaken loose, rolling away like gray bundles for ten or twenty feet before stopping, stunned and injured by the experience. But, as he took on real speed—as did the bikers in front of him, flying forward least they be caught in the path of the van barreling toward them—the race grew deadlier.

More rats came loose, the rage for human flesh having turned into blood-curdling terror as sharp, yellow-toothed mouths shrieked fearfully at the skies and beedy red eyes grew wide with horror, while dozens of bodies slipped off to be crushed under madly spinning wheels that squeezed flesh, blood, and entrails from furry skins like rotten bananas flying out of their peels, coloring the rocks red as severed tails flew in all directions. Then Stack sped up still more. Now, the final, most tenacious holdouts began to lose their grip under the overwhelming backflow of wind slapping against the van, tearing them off, twirling tails fluttering in the maelstrom before the beasts hit the asphalt with a splat and broke open, blood, innards, fur, flesh, and bones streaking the roadway.

By then the great mass of those which hadn't climbed onto the van were fleeing down the sharp sides of the drop into the narrow valley. Stack chose that moment to begin slowing down, beeping for the bikers up ahead to also put on the brakes, which they did.

When Stack came to a stop, he looked back at the now-empty road and shivered once before opening the van door and getting out on terra firma, his legs a bit wobbly under him. But Stack was tough. He quickly got himself under control. Courtner and the others came over. Courtner, his sandy hair waving in the wind, said, "Whew, that was a close one," then wiped sweat off his brow with his wrist in an exaggerated motion.

Stack, white as a sheet, said, "I thought for sure I was a goner when those bastards began to swarm over the van. I thought they'd find a way in, not sure if I'd closed off the openings. And then, when they were over all the windows so I couldn't see out, I thought for sure I'd go over the edge of the road and that would be the end of me. It's a miracle I got out of that one."

"Let's just hope we don't run into more rats," Courtner said.

"I can't guarantee what we'll run into," Stack told him. "This is a new world. A place no one's ever been to before. We don't know how many are dead or living, who's dying, what tomorrow will bring, or the extent of the damage to this country, Russia, or our NATO allies."

"It's not like opening the nightly news and listening to Dan Rather," Joe Angelicus said.

"No way," another biker added.

"Okay, boys," Stack finally said. "We can stand here, chewing the fat, discussing something that's gone and done, or we can get the hell down to the coast so what needs to be gets done."

"Which way do we go?" Angelicus asked. "Those rats might be waiting for us."

"I think not. Those bastards have had enough. If not, we can always go back the way we came. I'll go first and approach slowly. If things don't look kosher, I'll honk. You guys behind me can then turn around and head back. I'll follow and we'll find another route to the coast."

They all nodded to that, got on their bikes while he got back into his van, and then they moved forward, going slowly, watching warily for rats.

After a few hundred yards they saw the first dead, squashed animals, some still alive, lying on their sides, lifting their heads, noses sniffing the wind, high, keening cries rending the air, bloody wounds sticking some of the animals to the road. Others tried to move when they saw the van coming, but were unable to escape fast enough because of their wounds. The van went over some of the rats, blood, bits of fur, flesh, and guts flying in all directions as the hard, heavy wheels ground out what remained of rodent lives, drawing louder squeals of terror from the survivors. And a good number of them were now flattened by the motorcycles following along behind, a number of drivers aiming their bikes at certain rats on the road.

The van came to the place where Stack had put on speed and found more dead rodents, some flattened by the wheels which passed over them while others had been killed on impact as they came apart after hitting the road at 50 or 60 miles an hour when they fell from the van. The entire road along this stretch had been turned into a giant, surrealistic polka-dot painting. There were dozens upon dozens of splotches, sometimes one atop the other. In places the road was greasy, and Stack had to slow down to avoid skidding. Some rodents, which watched from the side of the road, had had enough and headed down into the safety of the steep valley.

When the convoy had moved past this point, it was clear sledding all the way to San Francisco. Signs of civilization became stronger, as well as zones of destruction. The intensity of the devastation increased as they came closer to the Bay Area. They spotted a long line of burned cars just off the road, with others scattered across an adjoining field, looking as if they had fled attacking fighter-bombers that came down to strafe from above. The vehicles had probably been caught by the intense heat flash of the nuclear explosions; 35 percent of the energy in any nuclear blast is expressed as an intense heat and light flash which can start fires up to 30 miles from the source of the explosion, depending on the size of the blast. And this phenomenon had probably caught these vehicles, setting off flammable materials inside and vinyl roofs topside, vaporing gasoline that quickly exploded or burst into flame with a power equal to hundreds of pounds of TNT, tearing out the guts of most vehicles, instantly killing the occupants with fire and a burst of schrapnel. Those cars had gone off the road immediately, probably crashing into other vehicles in the line of traffic. Still other cars, their drivers frantically trying to stop, had rolled into ditches. Now some of the occupants, blackened by flames, lay alongside their cars. Shattered windows showed the effects of internal blasts. And some vehicles, the drivers reacting in shock and panic, had driven up to a hundred feet off the road before being stopped by the terrain as their drivers died at the wheel. It reminded Stack of pictures he had seen of the Sinai passes after the Israeli Air Force had gotten through with the Egyptians in the 1967 War. The same hellish scenes. He could also smell the rotting flesh in the afternoon wind and see the clouds of flies around every car. Here and there he spotted rats skittering to and fro. What a fuck life was, he thought. Stack reflected a second on the mercy of God. Only he couldn't believe in it. Not then. Maybe what they said was true. That God made the world, then went off on an extended vacation.

The road was clear for the next half mile, then they passed farmland. Scorched fields, dead animals in the fields. Cattle and horses on their sides. A whole slew of chickens had fallen alongside a pond. Further back there were burned farm buildings and the bare outline of what had been a barn off to one side. Beyond were burned trees, then low hills and a blackened valley with burned groves of fruit trees. They moved from there through a small town with the roofs and top floors sheered off of buildings, debris-filled streets, burned bodies sticking out of the rubble, overturned cars and trucks. A few people picked through homes looking for valuables. None of them looked up as the convoy came through, moving around fallen bricks, broken glass, bits of furniture, and parts of cars.

The bikers were stunned by the sight, Stack not so much. He had been down to Fresno. They hadn't, and till now had been unable to picture a burned-out metropolis of 200,000 turned into a rubble ghost town. If this shocked them, they would be stunned by what would come later.

This town was on the periphery of the blast zone. Most of the buildings were standing and many hadn't been burned down. There were still people around, though it looked as if many had died and numerous others had left. For where he didn't know. Nor did Stack have time to reflect on what was happening. The momentum of events and the needs of the moment were pushing him along, forcing him toward set goals.

The bikers quietly followed the van, their eyes registering what they saw. Each of them—Courtner, Grushin, Angelicus, Phelan, Raussenbush, Stu Englund, Vance Chickering, Boozerton, Bonallila, Bill Ruald, Frank Dellatore, and Lou Senker—filed away in shock the details of destruction. And in the minds of many of them strong doubts about the survival of any of their blood kin began to grow. They had been aware that nuclear wars were massive killers and that few survived the hells which advanced technology had created. Yet there had been hope. Now, in the face of massive, crushing reality, a dark, growing depression began to sink down on their heads.

They left this town, and soon came to a suburban stretch with more burned cars and trucks, many of them off the highway, a number having crashed into one another in long, telescoped lines of wrecks in which some of the cars had been twisted like pretzels, sometimes two cars over, under, and around one another, with other cars sticking straight into the air, held up by the wrecks around them. The convoy moved past slowly, the men looking at this panorama of death, spotting bloodied heads and mangled bodies peeking out of smashed, open windows with lifeless, unseeing eyes. In vehicles where there had been fires, the faces sticking out were badly burned, teeth showing as if the skeletal remains were laughing at them. "Hey suckers, I'm dead. I'm free. But you're alive. You've got to fight and suffer and search and wonder about what the next dawn will bring." None of them knew what dead men did or didn't say, but that's how they imagined it. And since human imagination is a fertile and often deadly thing, what is hidden becomes a greater threat than the reality.

They came to a town much closer to the Bay. It was more devastated than what they had seen so far. The buildings, mostly single- and two-story jobs, wooden and sometimes brick, had, almost without exception, been sheered off at the base, the debris dumped into the cellars where many, having been warned over TV and radio about the coming war, had gone to hide from the bombs. Anyone hidden there was buried by a torrent of rubble. And then the fires had come, ignited by the detonations, almost simultaneously everywhere. How many had died in the flames and smoke, pinned by tons of rubble they couldn't escape, and were now being eaten by rats? Stack didn't know and didn't even want to estimate the toll. It hurt too much. The sight, the thought of it, was mind-numbing. Why the hell had he come out of the mountains? he asked himself. But Stack knew the answer. He had asked a foolish question to relieve the tension within, to create the fantasy possibility that he hadn't needed to come down here. But he had no choice in the matter if he wanted to go back East. And once there, he would only see more of this. Might as well get used to it.

They entered San Jose, which was even more destroyed, and stopped near the center of town, where they spotted a sheriff in a tattered uniform. He didn't even have a police car, just a beaten-up, dirty, old blue Dodge pickup. Stack parked nearby, got out, and went over to the lawman.

"Howdy. We're passing through and need some information."

"What do you need to know?" the sheriff asked in a hard, unfriendly voice which matched the look on his face. Having to see what he saw and having to do what he had done, Stack wouldn't have been any friendlier.

"We'd like to get to Sausalito to find the relatives of one of the men in our group." The sheriff looked for one moment at the bikers, then smiled grimly at Stack.

"That assumes they're still alive. But I guess it never

hurts to hope, though one shouldn't get one's hopes up too high. It won't be any better there than it is here. I hope you realize that."

"We're not fooling ourselves about anything," Stack answered as he took a longer look at the man beneath the veneer. This sheriff was tall, broad-shouldered, wide-chested, with a hard, rectangular face to match. A bad man to come up against anyplace, anytime.

"And how's the survival rate here in San Jose?"

"Look around. That should give you an idea. I doubt five percent survived. And many of them are now dead or on their way to the grave." He touched his chest briefly. "I'm the only surviving, intact lawman in these parts. And I'm not even on the San Jose police force. I'm sheriff in a town ten miles from here which no longer exists."

"What happened to the San Jose police?"

"Of the guys working the shift when the bombs went off, not one can be found. Those who weren't on duty either can't be found or are severely wounded. I've tried getting rescue operations going, while maintaining traffic control, and setting up food and water rationing. It's a hopeless task."

"Can you get outside help?"

"There's a military mission in San Francisco. I've tried to get them to come here. But they don't have the people, though they promised to try and get some volunteers here tomorrow. They're trying to mobilize what survivors there are in the National Guard. But first they've got to find them, and many of those still alive probably don't want to come. They've got their own troubles. As a result of all this, I've been able to do next to nothing. But a man's got to try. And as long as I'm at it, I might as well help get you to Sausalito safely.

"Your first problem is that many roads are impassable or no longer exist. Along with that, most bridges are gone. Either turned into chaff or scattered across the land and sea. Some, like the Golden Gate, are down in the water, blocking passage into or out of the Bay, except for small boats, which can make it through gaps in the structure. You can't cross to Sausalito from Frisco using the bridge. And if you try going around the long way from here through Fremont, then Hayward, San Leandro, Oakland, Berkley, and so on until you reach the Carquinez Toll Bridge, you've got nothing to cross. That's your first water barrier. Some miles to the east is another toll bridge which is also down. And should you make it across somehow, you then have the Napa River in the way, then more devastated land, then the Sonoma Creek, and finally the Pentaluma River, before you start heading down the peninsula to Novato, San Rafael, a few other burgs, and finally reach Sausalito. Of course, you can avoid all those water barriers if you go far enough east and north. But that merely makes your trek that much harder."

"What about boats? Can we make it by boat?"

"Sure," the sheriff said, his smile suddenly grim. "But go find one. The fires that burned so much, the blasts which turned so much into chaff, have not been any kinder to the boats, though you may find yourself one that's intact. Good luck. You and your friends will need it."

Stack's unsmiling face looked at the bikers. "Where do you want to go from here?"

Courtner wasn't one to dawdle. He said, "We can avoid the water barriers by going far to the east, then far to the north. But that's the long way around, and who knows how long our fuel will last and if we can get refills. Also, there may be barriers we don't know about. There are two choices left. We can go the long way around and cross all those water barriers, or into Frisco and cross the single water barrier between there and Sausalito. And once we get to the Bay it'll be easier to find someone to take us across once rather than again and again. Also, once in San Francisco, we'll be able to find some officer and tell him about the B-52."

The others nodded their approval of the plan, then Stack turned to the sheriff and asked the best way to get to San Francisco.

"Go up two blocks to Route 101, which goes to straight

to Frisco, except that part of it goes over water and may be out. When you pass San Francisco Airport on your right, take the first exit on the left, get onto Route 280, and follow that north into the city. Other than that, all I can say is the best of luck and I hope you find the people you're looking for.''

"Thanks," Stack and some of the others said. And then he got back into his van as they got back on their bikes. The sudden sound of motors starting up filled the air amid a cloud of acrid dust as they pulled out, quickly found a ramp onto Route 101, and headed toward San Francisco. But they were soon forced to slow down as they dodged wrecked, burned, smashed vehicles sprawled across the multi-lane roadway. Here, closer to the explosions, the harsh heat and fierce winds generated by the shock blasts had ripped out windows, turned over and twisted most vehicles, burned up everything in sight, while ripping off chunks of metal so that mangled pieces of every size, too numerous to count, covered most of the highway. They became an agony for the convoy turning this way, and still the convoy crunched over rubble.

Many vehicles lay amid blackened swaths where spilled fuel had burned a circle onto the highway. And inside each vehicle was the putrid horror of bodies turned into un-recognizeable lumps of meat which stank to high heaven and were covered with flies. From out of smashed windows, amid flies, roaches, and every kind of putresence one could imagine, rats grinned at them. Thousands of rats.

Horrified, the men proceeded, a cold numbness filling them, as it filled soldiers adjusting to the first terrors of combat. They sighted other cars, going in the same or the opposite direction, the drivers inside battered about, mostly in rags, some with burned faces, their cars as badly abused as they were, the paint mostly seared off, many without windows. Some waved at the convoy, but did not stop to talk. Strangers on this road of death, yet unified in a common bond of horrors shared.

3

They came to their first barrier, an overpass that had crashed down to the roadway below. They stopped, left their vehicles, and walked to the edge of the concrete chasm to look across at the continuation of the freeway 60 feet ahead, eyeing the thickness of jagged concrete and steel showing through like a sandwich bitten into by some nuclear giant. Even the steel barriers lining the freeway had been twisted and mangled like melted plastic which later cools.

They looked down. About 50 feet below great chunks of concrete were strewn about, and underneath lay crushed cars and trucks with gas tanks that had been punctured and ignited, burning to death any occupants who hadn't died under the fallen concrete. It was a harsh way to die, Stack thought. But in a violent world, he realized, few victims have the option of picking their own ends.

Courtner looked at Stack. "What now?"

"We should've expected this. If everything else got crunched, this freeway wouldn't be immune. Maybe where it runs along the ground it's useable, but not up in the air. There might be some exceptions, but this isn't one of them. We'll just have to backtrack till we find an exit, then get off, follow the freeway, and get onto the next ramp past this point."

They all agreed to that, then went back to their vehicles, turned around, and headed back, the rubble and vehicles looking slightly different from this direction. Soon, it started to seem like moving around boulders on some bad roadway, and they took it in stride. Courtner was amazed at how easily human beings adapted to the worst situations.

They quickly found an exit, took it, then moved along rubble-lined streets past burned-out, mostly deserted buildings of every type from office complexes to homes, warehouses, and schools. Then they passed a mostly intact government building, missing all its windows, like an old woman without any teeth. One could see the people who had rushed out where the front doors were missing. Burned, dying people who now lay sprawled across the front steps, then down the path to the sidewalk, many others on what had once been a front lawn, which was now burned black. The flesh had begun to rot and the whiff of putrid death touched the nostrils of the men riding past. Blackbirds were alighting on various bodies, chipping away at the flesh, then flying off to eat atop roofs or piles of debris or perhaps at some nesting place.

After moving through streets empty of all life, except for lone stragglers, to whom they waved and who sometimes waved back, they found an on ramp and were soon heading north on the freeway, going past the towns of Santa Clara, Sunnyvale, Mountain View, Palo Alto, and Menlo Park. They looked toward East Palo Alto and the bridge which had spanned the Bay from there, and saw that it was down in the water. The first of many downed bridges, they were sure.

They knew the names of some of the places they passed through, but not others, because signs had mostly been blown away. And since they were mostly strangers in this place, there were few landmarks known to them that had survived so that they might be able to orient themselves. Even men who had been this way before did not recognize the area. It all looked the same. Endless blackness, devastated rubble, missing roofs and upper floors. Where were the people? Dead, camouflaged among the debris, or had they fled for greener pastures?

The pattern of destruction changed from place to place. Wooden buildings were mostly gone, their locations signaled by large square or rectangular holes in the ground, filled with blackened rubble and, no doubt, the remains of people who had experienced firsthand the endless hells of fission-fusion power. As in Hiroshima and Nagasaki, those buildings made of brick or poured concrete and steel had kept their shape, and often stood like lone sentinels on a rubble horizon. But in many places even these had succumbed like mighty redwoods, only their steel girders still upright like exposed ribs on a body in which the flesh had rotted away. And all around one could see the piles of rubble formed into blocks, with the streets between like a grid of squares, rectangles, and triangles outlining the once-inhabited blocks. In places even the streets had disappeared.

Stack looked for nuclear bomb craters, but saw none. That meant there had been air bursts to maximize the destructive effect. Because of that the amount of rubble sucked up and radiation created had been considerably reduced.

To their right, as they passed Atherton, were fields of salt evaporators, and beyond them the Bay, strewn with the rubble of numerous pleasure boats. Some boats, where the water was shallow, stuck up out of the waves. There were also dead birds, many of them, floating on the water.

Now they came to another break in the freeway, where an overpass had been blown down. They left the highway and moved along it till they came to the Woodside Expressway, going west to the town of Woodside. This roadway was as different from the other as day from night, with fewer destroyed vehicles and less rubble. Perhaps there had been less traffic here when the bombs had gone off.

And now they began to see a lot more traffic. People in cars, trucks, even on bikes. There would be a lot more bikes as fuel sources dried up. Some people waved, others nodded. It was almost as if a certain camaraderie existed between survivors. A few did not wave at all, and moved along as if no one on that road existed but them, their faces troubled, their minds deep in thought.

They reached 280, but all on and off ramps, except for a few, were now rubble. After moving along for awhile, they found an intact ramp. As they got onto it, someone streaked by. A rider on a motorcycle without a helmet, wearing goggles, one hand on the handlebars, one hand holding a bottle of whiskey from which he took swigs, seemingly happy, giving out rebel yells, racing the wind and destiny, perhaps even death, or thinking he was. Some crazy guy unable to take the pressure of what had happened, Courtner thought to himself, while casting glances at the others, who cast them back. Stack realized the man was seeking an artificial glee by throwing his troubles into an alcoholic well. But that would only last till his liquor ran out, if he didn't crack up and kill himself first. And if he did live, when the liquor was gone the world would still be there, maybe worse than it now was, and he'd be a day older, though no wiser, or nearer to paradise or to the way things had been 73 short hours before.

They went past Redwood City and San Carlos. Both filled with fires for which there was no fire department to fight. Or, if there were, they had no water in underground pipes, only the possibility of bucket brigades. And it would take thousands to put out the flames in just one town. Stack doubted there was even a tenth of what was needed alive in either place. Most people, he was sure, were too injured, too sick, too stunned to help or give a damn.

To their right the San Francisco State Fish and Game Refuge stretched for miles. Much of it was burned, and those trees which had survived were leaning over 40 or 50 degrees from the vertical, away from the blasts that had occurred. Numerous birds had survived and flew in every direction. It was then that Stack and the others heard the shots and saw the many hunters moving through the reserve, firing at anything which flew or moved along the ground. The birds at least could fly, and if they were swift enough would live to see another day. Unfortunately for them, there would be men with guns in other places to hunt them as well. People were hungry and needed food. Game on the hoof and birds in the sky were the first available supply and targets of opportunity. Stack knew the amount of wildlife available couldn't supply the needs of the populace endlessly, even if only ten percent of the people survived, and he doubted it was that low. Animal life would run out if farming operations weren't sustained. Birds would survive the longest. Stack had read somewhere that the earth's bird population stood at around 100 billion. America had around seven percent of the land area, with more of it good for animal life than in mostly desert or arctic regions. So he guessed that ten percent of the world's birds lived in America, probably a fifth of that number in Alaska and the rest in the continental states. Despite the loss of most natural cover, birds, unlike other animal species, had not decreased vastly since Colonial times. Many now lived off garbage, like the gulls. But these thoughts flew from his head as more shots drew his attention back to the present.

"Dumb birds," he muttered as they flew in straight lines without weaving like fighter planes, making them easier to hit. He counted at least six falling from the sky as they flew off. But then they landed after a few hundred yards, only to be blasted by nearby hunters, so that they flew again, exhausted, frightened, their formations breaking in panic. As they did, more birds fluttered down in a flurry of blood and loose feathers as rifles tore gaps in their ranks while the birds fled the refuge, passing over the ruins of the town of Belmont. In its debris waited still more hunters. There was no rest for the fleeing victims. Gulls, starlings, geese, ravens, robins, anything and everything on the wing. The smallest bird could be plucked clean, thrown into the pot, and made into meat stew. Better a few nibbles than starvation.

Stack didn't want to look anymore. They were passing a large reservoir inside the refuge. People along the banks were taking out buckets of water. More still were fishing, many with homemade poles, trying to get something for themselves as well as those who depended on them.

The convoy passed this reservoir and another inside the refuge, then moved through San Bruno, where 280 became Junipero Sierra Boulevard and then a freeway. Twice they had to get off where overpasses had been blown down.

The men were by now exhausted. Tired of having to dodge rubble, dead bodies, turned-over, burned-out vehicles, getting onto and off freeways, looking out across blackened devastation, much of it monotonous—the way Europe had looked after World War II, only worse. At least there weren't any destroyed tanks to further mar the landscape, Courtner thought. But he had assumed this too soon. They passed an armory yard full of burned, smashed trucks, jeeps, M-113 armored troop carriers, and two M-48 Patton tanks partly flattened from the pressure of the bombs going off. One wall of the armory building still stood. The rest was debris.

They moved through a suburb known as South San Francisco, then Serra Monte, driving by the shopping center there, which was totally wrecked, with people going through the ruins looking for anything of value. After that, Daly City and Broadmoor were on their left. Then they entered San Francisco without knowing it since there were no street signs, with no difference in devastation from one place to the next.

San Francisco, City of Hills, colorful neighborhoods, Chinatown, the Mission District, Haight-Ashbury, Golden Gate Park, Fisherman's Wharf, the North Shore, Nob Hill, All history now. The destruction was vast, though not as massive as in Fresno. There were more large steel, concrete, and brick buildings here; plenty of them designed to withstand earthquakes and enough hills to deflect the blast of bombs, slowing down the power of winds shooting outward at thousands of miles an hour like shockwaves from the center of each explosion. Route 280, which cut through the city, had been terribly devastated, as overpasses had collapsed, sometimes one overpass onto another. They took the nearest exit and stopped atop one of the higher hills. Stack got out of his van and the others got off their bikes. They then stood in the middle of the street looking out at the thumb of San Francisco surrounded on three sides by choppy blue water, the collapsed Golden Gate Bridge to the north, the fallen San Francisco-Oakland Bay Bridge to the northeast. The docks along the northeast shore had been flattened into the water. The ships in dock at the time were either broken in half and turned into rubble, or shoved under the Bay, their mangled, burned superstructures still sticking out of the water. Stack tried to imagine how fiercely they had burned when their fuel had been ignited.

The water in all directions was covered by the floating debris of pleasure craft which had been destroyed, and which in numerous places peeked out of the waves near the shore. Those boats stored on land had been destroyed almost without exception. Looking across the Bay, one could see only a handful of motorized and sailing craft moving about.

Studying the landscape of the city, the men were shocked at how much smaller it seemed, almost like a lot stripped of trees or houses, Stack explained to the others that this was an optical effect. Bare land always looked smaller than it did when something stood on it.

Seeing the way it looked now, they tried imagining a pristine San Francisco, when it had been green and virginal and Indians lived on the peninsula, marred only by the occasional visiting whaler—Spaniard, Russian, or Mexican.

Finally, Stack said, "This is the end of one of the most beautiful cities in America. And to think I was here just a few days before it was wiped out. What a bastard life can be."

Joe Angelicus, having taken off his helmet, his short-cropped, curly black hair hanging down on his forehead, said, "I didn't realize what nuclear war meant till this moment. I knew it was bad, but not like this."

"Get used to it," Stack said. "Wherever you go, that's all you'll see."

"What do we do now?" Courtner asked.

"What I wanna do is rest my ass. I also want to eat. If you're hungry, the provisions Sheriff Willem provided are in the van. Bread, meat, bottled water, and soda in plastic two-liter bottles, though it's not cold. My suggestion is that we start gathering wood. We'll clear a place in the rubble, pile bricks around it, make a fire, and start cooking our meat. To do that we'll need a sheet of metal to cook it on. I only have pots or pans for two men at a time. If we look around, we should find a piece of metal we can wash off, then burn over the fire to purify before we use its surface as a grill."

Having said that, Stack headed into the ruins to the right, motioning to one of the bikers, a man by the name of Dellatore, to come with him. Dellatore, short, slim, dark, tough-looking, followed him over a pile of bricks, then through a gap in a half-collapsed wall into a building with roof and innards gone, and from there into an extensive yard.

They came to a large, intact wall covered with graffiti from another time and place. In blazing red letters now almost burned off were two words: TOTAL ANARKEE. A twisted spelling of the word anarchy, which said a lot about the present world. And next to that, RONALD RAY GUN, a pithy comment about a past President whose politics the left had not liked. It made Stack wonder, if America had been stronger, whether all this would have happened. No, he told himself, and silently cursed what the left had done to the country in their endless orgy of emasculation.

They moved past this wall to one which had partly caved in, and entered the gutted ruins of what had been a showroom with a once-huge display window. Then they stopped. Across the street, huddled against the wall of a six-story government building, were what looked to be blackened cylinders.

"Is that what I think it is?" Dellatore asked.

"Yeah," Stack said, remembering his first reactions down in Frescno. He looked briefly at Dellatore, whose eyes were wide with shock as his nostrils flared with exploding emotions, then back at the wall again.

These had once been people, perhaps running for the relative safety of the office building. But they didn't make it in time. The bombs went off first. The horrid flash of fire, the ruthless nuclear light, and they cringed, then fell back and flattened out against the wall, one staggering into the other, perhaps forty people in all. And that's how they were fused to the concrete. Turned into charcoal. Some spreadeagled as if crucified, others huddled, shoulders down, arms around loved ones. He could see gaping holes where mouths had cried out one last time before being stilled forever. Clothing was gone. Naked feet had been soldered to the sidewalk. Human forms, barely recognizeable now, were exposed to the gaze of all; obscene sculptures in charcoal like those one saw popping out of the wall on some national momument depicting hundreds of characters in some great and epic battle.

"It's horrible," Dellatore stuttered, not yet having been numbed to the same degree Stack had. "How could such things happen? How could God allow it?"

"I don't know, mister. I wish I could say it's all a great mystery and that he'll make it all well in the end. But that doesn't quite wash in my book. All I can say is that the Old Boy isn't as good or merciful as his commercials in the Bible make him out to be. I'm sorry I can't be more positive and not sound blasphemous, but I'm all out of righteous belief after what's gone down."

"I don't condemn you," Dellatore said, looking at Stack suddenly, his eyes a startlingly bright blue. "I come from a religious family. My mother, bless her soul," he crossed himself, "if she were still alive, would have had something to say to you. Not me. I wasn't much for religion before this, and I don't think I'm going to go in that direction now. Not after this." He gestured at the devastation.

"How do you know your mom's dead? She might still be alive."

"Perhaps you misunderstood. She's been dead over seven years now. Long before this horror. Cancer did her in. She was sixty-three when she died. That woman could've lived fifteen, maybe twenty years more if not for the cancer."

"And she kept her faith, even through all that shit?"

"Yeah, with some people it makes them more religious. They say it's all in God's hands and maybe they're going to meet him."

"I'm not that way. I say to God, you fuck me and it's all over. I'm not your dart board. You want me to show love and respect, treat me in a way that will merit it. Love has to be earned, even by a God. You may find my attitude brazen and hard, but I think even so small an object as a human being, while showing some respect for God and asking for his mercy, has to draw the line somewhere. This far and no further, even for the Master of the Universe. One should be as good a son to God as he is a father to us. It's a two-way street."

"I'll have to think that over," Dellatore said.

"You do that. And now let's go find that sheet metal. Our hungry boys are waiting to eat. And while the horrors won't go away, people have to eat to preserve their strength."

They began to look around and, after a minute or so, Dellatore saw what they wanted sticking up from a rubble hill. "There," he said excitedly.

Stack looked at where Dellatore was pointing and both men hurried over, rushing up the rubble slope, wobbling unsteadily as broken bricks and partly burned planking shifted under their feet. But they made it and began to tug at the sheet, scooping and pulling away bricks and wood and concrete dust until the metal was loose enough to pull out.

"It's dirty as hell," Dellatore said.

"Don't matter," Stack answered. "We'll wash it off, wipe it clean, and purify it over a fire first."

Just then they heard shots and the sounds of someone running—their way.

4

The two men looked up from the large, flat metal square they had been tugging on and out at the street, past where the picture window had been. A man was racing uphill, gut-wrenching fear on his face. Farther back, almost invisible, a man stopped, aimed, and fired. His rifle went off and a bullet dug into rubble by the side of the road. His enthusiasm was obviously greater than his skill.

The running man, his shoulder-length blonde hair flopping in the wind, rushed in through the opening to the showroom just as another round came flying past, closer this time, sending up debris a foot from the runner's legs. The runner, now red in the face, his eyes wild as he fled for his life, spotted Stack and Dellatore and stopped for one second in shock, thinking that part of the pursuit group had moved around to catch him from in front.

"Quick, this way," Stack said, having spoken as if the words came from somewhere deep inside and another person was controlling him.

The blonde man rapidly realized they were not enemies, but potential victims like himself, and ran toward them.

"This way, this way," Dellatore said, leading the way back to where the others were. They moved swiftly, seemingly running on angels' wings as if their feet weren't touching the ground as they moved over and between piles of debris. And they didn't stop till they reached the sidewalk where the others were gathering wood and bricks.

"What the hell's happened?" Courtner questioned when he saw them. Then he looked at the third man. "And who's he?"

"I don't know," Stack gasped. "All I do know is that someone with a gun is chasing him." Stack hooked a thumb in the direction from which they'd come. All three were breathing so hard they could barely talk.

Stack didn't waste any more time as he ran to the van to get his rifle. The bikers who'd helped defend the B-52 went for their guns. By then Stack was back with his weapon and several clips of ammunition and heading in the direction from which he'd come. On reaching a low section of a nearby wall, Stack dropped down and looked back at the bikers advancing cautiously. Then he stared briefly at the blonde-haired man, hidden behind a low rubble mound, the fear visible on his face now formed into a rictus of death, his body trembling so much that he resembled a spastic.

Stack turned back around and waited for the attacker to appear. He did, or rather two of them did. One was a tall, hard-faced, foreign-featured man with a hawk nose, sharp features, and watchful eyes that looked as if they had seen a lot of evil. The other man was fat, with too much gut and long blonde hair partly held in place by a red and white polka-dot bandanna around his forehead. Both held rifles and moved carefully, eyes scanning the terrain. Then they spotted Stack, and he called out to them to halt and drop their weapons.

They responded by throwing themselves down behind separate cover and began to fire. Incoming rounds thunked into the wall Stack was behind, sending chunks of brick and dust flying. The sharp, flat crack of their guns spoke of the power in their control and their willingness to use it. But more than two could play that game. Stack gave as good as he took, even better.

He exposed a fraction of his head, letting one eye skim what was out there, and saw the blonde-haired attacker, his big beer belly exposed, getting up to move toward the next rubble mound. As he started to make his move, Stack loomed up and fired. Perhaps too fast. His bullet struck two feet away from the blonde man, who fell back behind the cover he had been leaving as a smashed brick flew in two directions.

The fat man, behind cover now, looked over at the Iranian who had directed this attack. The Iranian signaled that all would be made good. Was he not a veteran of the Battle of the Howazaya Marshes in the Great Iran-Iraq Gulf War? He had boasted that he had the military experience to come out the victor against any foe in combat.

Stack tried to look out, but was forced to pull back because of incoming fire from the Iranian's side. To get around that, Stack moved along the wall, out of view, hoping to pop up where his enemy wasn't expecting him to give him a hello he wouldn't forget. At the same time some of the bikers, Joe Angelicus in particular, started pegging shots at where the fat blonde man was hidden as they reached the wall. Slugs tore into brick, into wood, into metal, ricocheting, sending chunks of brick, wood, and metal flying in all directions, causing the fat man to panic. He tried to rise and fire in order to make it hot for his attackers and alleviate the pressure. Instead, a bullet struck him in the left shoulder. With a shriek, he dropped his rifle and rolled down to the bottom of the rubble pile he had been using as cover; groaning heavily now, one hand over the wound which was gushing blood and burned into him as if some poker out of hell had been rammed deep into the muscle, then down through the bone to the very center of the marrow. In response, fires of pain in photon blasts of endless intensity shot up and down his arm, into his chest, radiating across it, touching every internal organ so that they vibrated with sympathetic pain and made his heart feel as if pincers were jabbing it all over, sending the blood pumping harder through him to press down against the wound, which telegraphed another series of pains across his body till he thought he would faint, as flashes of purple fire danced behind his eyes and made him think for long seconds that he was going blind.

As this was happening and attentions were diverted, Stack popped up and caught the Iranian. On instinct alone, without any fancy aiming, he pumped three shots, all at skull level, toward the Iranian. Two of the bullets zinged into the mound he was behind, but the third struck home. It was a lucky shot, and half an inch to the right would have missed altogether. But it didn't miss. The bullet tore off the Iranian's left ear, sending a gusher of blood flying outward from the side of his head in a sudden half-globe burst of flying red droplets.

The Iranian recoiled in the opposite direction and grabbed for the side of his head. Stack cautiously peered over the top of the wall, and then he and the others—Angelicus, being the bolder, leading them—advanced toward the debris mounds behind which the two attackers lay. They moved up, over, and around the mounds, closing in on the wounded blonde man and the Iranian, who shivered in agony, holding the bleeding gash where his ear had been, the ear lying in a rippled mass of reddened flesh a foot from where his head had popped up. The Iranian did not move as they hovered over him. He continued to lie in a fetal position, groaning in pain and shivering in visible discomfort.

"Who are you?" Stack asked the Iranian. But the man was in too much pain to answer anything. Stack looked over at the other man. Angelicus was questioning him and he was talking, though visibly in pain.

"My name's Cuttman," he said. "I was a longshoreman before the war." Then he stopped speaking as his face twisted up in a spasm of pain.

"Who's the other guy?" Angelicus asked.

"Mohammed something or other. I don't know his full name. Something Arabic or Iranian. God," he added as he folded in deep pain, then twisted about in agony. "I need help. Wounded bad," he groaned.

"I'll just go to the nearest phone booth and call a

hospital," Angelicus grimly joked.

"There is a medical facility near here," the man who had been chased by the two wounded assailants announced as he came forward from behind the mound where he had hidden during the gunfight. All eyes turned to him except those of the Iranian, who was still holding himself in agony and probably also in shock.

"There's a medical emergency center, sort of, in the Candlestick Park area southeast of here. I was there once when I brought in some injured friends. Don't get me wrong. It's no hospital. The park is a mess. The stadium's a shambles. But inside the stadium are whatever medical personnel and facilities still exist in this city. The military's set up a base there and organized things."

"Are there a lot of wounded in the facility?" Stack asked.

"Hundreds. Who knows? I didn't count 'em."

"A lot of medical personnel?"

"Dozens, maybe more. I didn't survey the place. I just dropped off my friends and returned to the people I'm with."

"You're part of a group?"

"Yessir."

"Where are you staying?"

The blonde man pointed east. "About ten, twelve blocks that way. Our group lived behind a big hill that shielded us from the light, heat, and blast of the bombs to a fairly good degree. The area's still pretty messed up, but not as bad as some places which were wiped clean. We lost some people, but most survived, a goodly number of them injured. Those were mostly minor injuries: scratches, bumps, bruises, that sort of thing. We're now living underground in a new place we found."

"Okay. Now can you tell me why these two dudes," Stack hooked a thumb at them, "were trying to off you?"

"It's like this," the blonde man said, shifting uneasily. "There are these radical Iranians and Arabs in the country. Some were attending Berkley, others worked in various places. After the bombing they began to claim surviving homosexuals in this area were spreading AIDS, which would further effect an already weakened population. People are scared as hell and this made things worse. They've helped organize a posse which has been killing gays and anyone they think looks gay. I'm not gay, but I'm part of what used to be a community of hippies with roots in this city. That seems just as bad to these people. There ain't no law to stop 'em. The law disappeared with the bombings. I never thought there'd come a day when I'd miss the police.''

The blonde man paused to scratch his hair. Stack saw he was balding around the crown of his head and his hair was streaked with gray. He estimated the blonde man was 43, maybe 44. His face had the gaunt look of many who live the communal kind of life. That mixture of wisdom, experience, hope, naivete, disappointment, radicalism, utopia, and loss. And now it had all come to this.

"We're taking you with us," Stack said. "No use leaving you here to possibly get snuffed by their friends. Maybe we can find some military personnel to help you out of your dilemma."

"Thanks, mister. But we already tried and couldn't get them to help."

"Let me try, What's your name, by the way?"

"Dean Bushnell."

"Okay, Dean. My name's Stack. Nick Stack. The guys with me are from a Harley-Davidson bike club. Good guys, not hoodlum bikers. That one there's Bay Courtner, leader of the group.'' Bushnell nodded to the sandy-haired man with the small mouth and spade jaw. The others said their hellos, then Stack began directing the placing of the wounded into his van.

The Iranian and Cuttman cried out in horrid pain and bled harder as they were lifted. But there was no choice. They had to be moved. Stack grimaced as he thought of the floor of his van being covered with blood.

The bikers placed the two wounded men, now crying out

loudly, in the back of the van as gently as possible. There was no ambulance service or paramedics as such, and if they didn't do the moving these men would bleed to death. And the two wounded men would just have to rough it as they traveled to the emergency center the way so many Contras and Afghan freedom fighters had done in years past.

Things were pushed out of the way to make more room in back. Then Bushnell was told to get in with the wounded men to see to it that they didn't bump themselves too badly. Stack had to drive and the bikers had to ride their motorcycles.

Bushnell didn't feel like playing nursemaid, but had no choice and complied. The guns and ammunition the wounded man had brought with them had already been divided among the bikers. The convoy now started off in the direction toward which Bushnell had pointed them.

They moved at no more than 20 miles an hour, slowing down to avoid rubble and burned vehicles in the street, sometimes climbing over debris and coming back down with a bump which shook the van and made the men in back groan aloud. Bushnell looked at them and grinned at what they were going through. It made him feel better about his ordeal.

Stack looked back a moment and asked, "Are you watching them?"

"Sure," Bushnell answered, and hid his inner glee. They went past a block of six-story apartment buildings. The rears had been caved in, but the fronts looked fairly intact if one ignored the missing windows and the strands of curtains hanging out. The convoy then went down a wide boulevard, followed by a narrow street of private houses which had been sheared off at ground level filling the cellars with blackened rubble.

They arrived at Candlestick Park sooner than expected. The stadium was in a large open area. Stack did not know if that was how it had looked before the war, or if the bombs had eliminated most of the surrounding cover.

There were many burned-out cars in what looked to be parking lots. The debris lying all around could have been created locally or blown in from miles away.

The stadium itself was still fairly intact and looked as if it had ridden out the nuclear storm quite well. But then they got closer and saw the beams and concrete chunks and various pieces of metal all around the grounds and hanging from the outside walls.

Bushnell led them to an empty area on the other side of the stadium. Beyond it they saw what had once been docks and were now mostly sunken sections under the choppy blue of the Bay. Farther distant were the seemingly serene faces of communities on the opposite shore and the high ground beyond. But fires could be seen across the land; endless campfire pillars of black and low-hanging smoke smog extended over the face of the waters.

Going around the curve of the stadium wall to the right, they saw the start of the medical emergency facilities, people being brought in or out, lines of wounded, or perhaps dead, along the outside stadium wall. They couldn't be sure from the distance.

The convoy moved slowly and steadily across the open, flat, sometimes scorched area, then stopped as they came near the entrance through which the casualties were being taken in or released. Stack spotted a grimy-looking paramedic and called out to him. The man, in his mid-20s, was standing to the side and having a smoke, perhaps also a rest between labors.

"Yeah, can I help you?" he asked, his face none too eager.

"I've got some wounded in here. Who's in charge of taking care of the injured?"

"Anyone who comes to get them."

"Where are those anyones? Who do I see?"

The guy standing there smoking his butt had a kind of funny look on his face as if all this amused him in some strange way. Perhaps as if he were a scientist looking at the world under a microscope. It was obvious the war had affected him and now he was incapable of dealing with this tragedy unless he treated it as he did. Having reasoned this through, Stack decided to take things into his own hands and not let events move him along as he got out of the van and headed for the entrance into the stadium, the entrance doors now gone and lying on the ground nearby.

Along the hallways inside, the paint had been almost scorched off the walls. There were people in every direction, lying on the floor, sometimes on stretchers, but mostly on bare concrete. Others sat against the walls, most of them glassy-eyed.

Stack went left, looking up, noticing there was no electricity and that the only light was a dim grayness filtering in from outside. He passed a stairway leading up into the stadium. Sitting on the steps were injured and disgusted people, some of them talking, but most looking out at the world with empty eyes, perhaps lost in their own thoughts. Like troops who've lost a battle going over the moves of what they'd done, trying to find where they'd failed and what different moves might have made it all go right. But in this case no move was the right one. The weapons of war were too overwhelming.

Stack spotted a side room down a short hall to the right. It was filled with badly wounded, and a harried doctor in his late 40s, maybe early 50s, with straggly gray hair, was working hurriedly, with the assistance of two nurses, on a young boy of 11 or 12, still conscious but in shock, his chest looking crushed, his breathing stertorous. Stack saw no intravenous plastic bags, no lifesaving equipment, only the most rudimentary items. The shocking sights gave him a powerful feeling that this boy was going to die.

"Sir," Stack said, his voice failing him, "I've just driven here with two wounded men in my van. Both suffering from bullet wounds."

The head did not turn for a second. When it did, the face that looked at him was pained, harassed, full of disgust. "Wounded, you say?" Stack nodded. "Bullets?"

"Yeah. One's mine. They attacked us. But that's

another story. The fact is they're here and bleeding badly."

"Can't do anything about it. I'm too involved here." He looked down at the boy on the table, then at one of the nurses, an older woman in her 50s. "Nurse Lepp, would you please go with this gentleman and see how the wounded are, then report back here."

"Come on," she said, her hard-rock, pioneer-type voice not too friendly. But something about her manner indicated she was a person used to taking charge, giving her orders, and operating with a certain efficiency and direction. Stack guessed she had been a head nurse once.

Stack led her to the van. Nurse Lepp looked at the men, did some probing, asked some questions, and took pulses while the men gasped in agony. Cuttman was able to answer reasonably well when asked questions, but the Iranian was in complete shock by now.

Stack stood to one side holding one of the van doors, though they didn't need holding. Then Nurse Lepp turned around, saw the young man Stack had asked for help, and in a loud voice called out, "Elroy, come over here." He came immediately, without hesitation, or even the hint of a smile.

When he arrived at the rear of the van, she said, "Go get some men and stretchers. These two are in a very bad way and need a doctor. See if Doctor Halpin is available." Elroy disappeared into the stadium at a run.

"How long's this place been used as a hospital?" Stack asked.

"A day and a half. Almost every hospital's been knocked down, burned to the ground, or so badly damaged that there's nothing left to treat and keep patients in. This being one of the better-preserved places, it's being used on orders of the National Guard."

"They're in charge?"

"Just about. They're the law." By then Elroy was running back with a stretcher. Behind him came three more men, one holding another stretcher. They moved with an economical sort of hurry, knowing this was the kind of work they would have to repeat over and over, also knowing they couldn't keep up the rapid pace endlessly. So they employed the most economical hurry they could afford to and still live. Their faces had that tense, anxious look of soldiers at war. Men knowing they hadn't a sparrow's chance of survival if they didn't watch every step they took. Their eyes were just as watchful as those of combat soldiers, one eye on the job ahead, one eye on the surrounding terrain, flitting this way and that. The stretchers they carried were of the wooden-pole-and-canvas variety. Cheap, primitive, but effective.

Behind them, running a bit slower, in dirty white pants, a filthy white jacket, and a green surgical shirt covered with blood spots, came Doctor Halpin. A blonde, blue-eyed man, around 28, wearing glasses and looking almost as grim as the scene around them.

He went into the van first as the others parted and let him through. Two quick examinations determined the state of things to come. He turned to one stretcher team. "Take the dark-skinned man to Room 7B. The blonde one goes to Room 4A." He looked at Cuttman. "Do you know your blood type?"

"I dunno, man."

"Great. We'll just have to give you Type AB. That's good for everybody. And if there's time, we'll check your blood type and maybe match you up with somebody."

"Will I live, Doc?" Cuttman gasped, a worried look on his face.

"Nobody dies from an arm shot. And the other guy won't die either, but both of you will suffer a lot."

With that, he stepped from the van so the stretcher people could do their work. Then he looked at Stack and the bikers standing nearby.

"You with these two gentlemen?" he asked none of them in particular.

"Sort of," Stack said, and reported what had gone down.

"Nice guys," Halpin replied. "After years in this business little surprises me. I wish I could continue this chat," he said, "but duty calls."

"One more thing," Stack added. "Where is the honcho in charge of this operation—the military end, I mean?"

"He should be somewhere inside. Maybe out on the ball field. He's a big, rawboned man about yay big." Halpin lifted his arms to the six-foot-two level. "About yay wide," he added, indicating football shoulders. "Blue eyes, strong jaw, bony nose, cold, blue eyes, dark brown, graying hair. More gray than brown. Big head and an ego to match. His name's Callister. Colonel Wayne Callister."

"Gotcha," Stack said as Halpin turned and headed back inside. Halpin hadn't slept for almost 80 hours. Yet somehow he was only partly numb and still able to function. He hadn't stopped treating the dying and injured since after the war began. With the poor selection of tools at hand, he was losing far more people than would have been the case in a more prepared and modern facility. But given the circumstances that existed, he wasn't doing that badly.

For one second, as he headed down halls full of wounded and dying, his mind skimmed back to the way things had been before the war. Finished with his residency, earning 80 grand a year, looking forward to more, smug and proud of his achievements, he had had just one blot on his record. The wife he had married some years earlier, who had made his life hell. Anorexic bitch, he thought, a bitter smile momentarily creasing his features. But then he remembered how he had rushed home when he'd come out of the shelters, after the initial bombing was over, and found his house wrecked and his wife dead. Not under the rubble. No. But burned like a rag doll, her arms spreadeagled, almost as if some huge ornament hung there, blown by the force of the blast through a wall into the bathroom, where she was fused to the wall over the wreckled toilet bowl. What a fitting end for a bitch who had made his life hell. He knew he was thinking things that were terrible, but no longer gave a damn. She was the past now. Gone forever. Thank God and good riddance. All he had left was the present, which slowly and relentlessly marched into the future, dragging him and a thousand others with it.

5

Stack headed back into the stadium and onto the scorched playing field, looking around at the bleachers, which in many places had been torn from their moorings in a rain of debris that covered almost everything. Scavengers, who had gathered wood wherever it was to be found, were making campfires in the corners of the field and cooking meals.

The colonel, in the center of the field, stood out in a crowd. One, for his physical appearance. Two, because of his uniform and the jeep he was standing next to while talking over a field radio. Stack walked over and waited till Callister was finished.

He put the mouthpiece down, looked at Stack, and asked, "Yes, can I be of help?" He said it in a hard, no-nonsense way, eager to meet and solve this problem so he could go on to the next one.

"My name's Nick Stack. I've come down from the mountains east of Fresno where a B-52 with engine problems landed on a deserted airfield. It was unable to complete its mission and couldn't return to its destroyed base. A biker gang, in the area at the time, took over a town, which I and others helped liberate, and attempted to grab the B-52 and its load of bombs, which we prevented. The bomber's now under guard, full of lethal weapons, unable to complete its mission or make radio contact with some outside command. That's why I was sent here to find someone to get word up the chain of command, so some airbase can send mechanics to repair the plane and it can, if needed, complete its mission.''

"Where's the field? Who's the plane's commander?''

"The valley's maybe thirty miles east of the town of Vista Royale. The commander's Giles Garudet out of March Airfield in southern California.''

"I know where that is. Now I'll try to get the message out. The problem is that due to heavy static we can only send over short distances, and the message is then passed in that manner from set to set.'' Callister got back on the field phone as Stack took a cigarette from his almost empty pack.

After a number of tries, Callister got some colonel on the line, repeated a condensed version of what he'd been told, then listened some, said a few more words, hung up, and turned to Stack. "Your message got through the first rung of the communications ladder. How long it'll take to get where it should, who'll get it, who'll take responsibility and send help—I don't know and can't say. I'm just one cog in a very big, badly damaged wheel.''

Callister took out a bent pack of cigarettes, put a butt between his teeth, balanced it there as if it were a cigar, then lit it with an old World War II Zippo lighter.

"What were you doing up in the mountains that got you into this situation and how did you find out about me?''

"I'm from back East, New York. I came to San Francisco on business, then decided to top it off by taking a break—camping, fishing, and hunting in the mountains when the war began. I immediately headed for the nearest civilization, ran into a young hitchhiker, came to the town of Montieth, and got involved with the people in the area. Their problems became mine. All the while I looked for a way to get back East. I wanted to drive, but with the shortages of repair facilities, fuel, and all the devastation, that might have gotten me into worse trouble. So I began looking for a way to catch a flight going east.

"To more specifically answer your second question, I

went down to Fresno to try and find the parents of the hitchhiker I picked up. They were no longer around, but once there I found the guy in charge of medical evacuation, a Major Bill Bathhurst, who told me he was down there from his main HQ in San Francisco, which is how I knew about your command.''

"Bill Bathhurst?" Callister said, smoke jetting from his mouth and nostrils. He was suddenly more friendly. They had an acquaintance in common. "Bill's in my personal command.''

"It's a small world," Stack said in surprise.

"Yeah, too small almost. Bill's coming here soon on twenty-four hours' leave, so he can find his family.''

"When he arrives, tell him I'm here. I'd like to see Bill. I owe him one. He helped the people with me in their hour of need and I'd like to return the favor and help him find his people now—if they're alive.''

"I'll let him know. But where will you be? There's an awful lot of rubble out there to get lost in. Tens and tens of thousands of acres. It's amazing how much men and women have built up over the years. And all that work made useless in so short a time.'' His face momentarily grew sad as he hung his head. But then he looked up again, hard, his bony face a mask of military toughness. And Stack respected him for it.

"Yeah. It's a bitch of a mean thing to swallow. I'm still reeling," Stack said.

"So's everyone, mister. Devastation on such a scale is hard for any human to fathom.''

"You're right. But we have to carry on. There's no choice if we want to go on living. However, to get back to what we were talking about, I really don't know how he can contact me. I've got places to go and things to do. But I will be back this evening.''

"What places and what things?''

Stack quickly told him about what had transpired and that he was going to see about the safety of the people involved, but that they needed help.

"Mister, there's nothing I can do. I've already been asked. I'm barely able to help people trapped under rubble, old people unable to get down from their third-floor apartments because the stairways in their buildings are gone and there's no elevator service."

"You won't help at all?" Stack asked, disappointed in Callister for the first time.

The colonel fastened those frosty blue eyes on Stack and said, "Look, it's not that I don't want to. I haven't the people I need. I'm a colonel. I should have two or three thousand people in my command. I don't. I'm working with a skeleton force to try and save lives. As it is, I know most won't last till we finally get to them. There's nothing I can do for your victims. They can't be my concern. Let them fight, or move away from the danger." He paused. "Let me do this another way. I'm deputizing you, mister, and those with you. We'll give you some guns and ammo and then you can go and protect these people. Fair?"

"But we've got other things to do."

"Don't you want to help?"

"Sure."

"Then do this."

"But we have people to find, relatives of one of the men in the motorcycle club I came down from the mountains with."

"That's been pre-empted. It can wait for later. Your country needs you. Have you been in the service?"

"Yes. The National Guard."

Callister grinned. "My branch. Back in New York State, I suppose."

"That's right."

"So you know what serving your country means and the importance of priorities."

Stack looked down at the burned turf, then back at Callister. "Yes, I do. But the men with me will be disappointed."

"They'll just have to wait a while longer. Then I'll release them to go do what they have to."

"I don't know if you can legally do this."

"Probably not. But look around. The world's been turned upside down on its head. In such a world extraordinary conditions exist. And extraordinary conditions call for extraordinary measures."

"I understand, colonel. In your place I'd have done the same, maybe worse."

"Glad we have a meeting of the minds."

"I'll go tell those who came with me. But whatever happens, I'll be back. So tell Bathhurst to wait."

"You're doing a lot of helping, mister. I hope someone will help you get back East to find your family, assuming they're still around."

"I realize the possibility of their being gone. But I'm willing to chance it. Now let me talk to the others about the change in plans. Then I'll get back to you about the ammo and weapons we'll need."

Stack hurried across the field, then through the corridor to the outside. The sight of wounded people in pain, people hurrying past, and others stunned almost out of their minds became a swift blur, not even enabling him to focus on one image before the next visual object took its place.

He was soon back at the van where the others waited, some of them smoking or talking to Bushnell. When Stack appeared the talking stopped as they gathered around him in a half circle, waiting to hear what had happened. Stack told them what Colonel Callister said when he asked for help.

"It's up to us?" Bill Ruald, a stocky, grayish-blonde man asked in shock.

"That's right. I know we had other plans, but the colonel's changed our direction temporarily and he is the law around here. Besides, if we don't help when we have the power to do so, this guy here," he looked at Bushnell, "and all his people could be in extreme danger. Even if they run, there's no guaranteeing the mob won't follow them, then carry out a massacre. We stopped evil in the mountains and now should help end it here.''

Ruald spoke again. ''I understand what you're saying. But there's a limit to what we can do. We're only thirteen men. Now I won't comment on that being an unlucky number. But even if each of us was ten times better than we are, we still couldn't fight the world, nor should we have to.''

''I'm not suggesting we even fight one percent of the world. But we have to do something. We can't just desert this man. More than that, we have to obey the orders of the authority in command. If each of us begins pulling in different directions the world will descend into a jungle. I know it's hell now, but it can become even worse. So far we've been badly shaken, but the Russians haven't taken our souls, our sense of dedication to duty.''

''Okay,'' Ruald said, looking at the others for confirmation. ''We'll do it. But then we go look. For Tom Grushin's people. I suppose after that,'' he looked at Stack, ''you'll return to the mountains.''

''Yes,'' he said, thinking also of the help he was going to give Bathhurst. But he didn't tell them that. With everything else they had to do, this might make them reject the whole proposal. When Bathhurst went looking for his people, Stack would volunteer to go along and ask the others to join him.

Everything having been decided, he went back to see Callister, who was on the field radio again. Stack waited till Callister was finished, told him everything had been agreed to and that now his men needed the guns and ammo they'd been promised. Only half were armed. And they would also need weapons for the volunteers among those being attacked.

Callister said they could have what they needed. There were more weapons than men left to use them. The colonel turned to his aide, a lanky farmboy by the name of Clinton Bainbridge, and told him to take Stack to a locked room in a sublevel of the stadium. Inside were boxed rifles, boxes of bullets, clips, even grenades. The National Guard hadn't come empty-handed. They were prepared for every contingency. Stack looked around while Bainbridge shone a flashlight over the arms trove. He finally chose a dozen M-16 rifles, 300 rounds for each gun, enough to fill ten clips, plus half a dozen grenades for each man in the group. That would be enough to take care of those enraged survivors of the war who'd succumbed to homophobia and an illogical fear of AIDS.

Knowing what the epidemic had been doing to the public before the war, Stack could understand the fear. People had listened to the reports on TV and radio and read the papers and magazines, as an ever-mounting toll took more and more victims and various drugs, hailed as wonder weapons, proved ineffective, or of only limited help. The number of infected people in the United States had risen past 60,000, then 80,000, and finally 100,000, moving out of the gay and drug-user communities. Over 50,000 victims lay in the ground, and the numbers infected was increasing at the rate of a thousand a week. It was frightening, threatened a more terrifying future. And the war had exacerbated every horror to a ruthless level of savagery.

Bainbridge and Stack, both carrying heavy loads, came upstairs and moved along corridors thick with wounded and dying, then out to the van. There, the men looked over the supplies, and those without guns picked up rifles, loaded them, and fired a few rounds at a nearby rubble heap to acquaint themselves with their weapons. At the sound of shots, everyone came running to find out what had happened.

Stack looked at Bushnell. "The remaining guns and ammo are for your people so you can defend yourselves."

Bushnell looked at the guns with distaste. "Why? Can't the colonel send troops to defend us?"

"You heard what went on. He doesn't have the man-power. This is in our hands and yours now."

Bushnell did not look too happy. Stack read him for one of those leftist liberals who, before the war, had assailed the military establishment and now expected them to unswervingly fight for him.

"I know what you're thinking," Stack said. "But this time you're going to have to dirty your hands. You can't hide from reality forever. It's a tough world out there and you're going to have to learn to cope, mister."

Bushnell didn't say anything as Stack loaded the van with guns and ammo, then told everyone it was time to get going. He thanked Bainbridge for his help before the other man returned into the stadium. As he did so, Stack and Bushnell got into the van, then drove off, followed by the bikers.

As they moved out, they went past a small pickup with four rear-mounted searchlights on a stand. Each searchlight was the size of a small oil drum. They looked more modern than the World War II-type searchlights one saw in old combat film footage and at movie premieres.

Bushnell pointed at the searchlights and at the rubberized arms which swiveled them about and served as a conduit for the energy flow which kept them lit.

"They use those at night and twirl them this way and that to let anyone who needs to come here find his way. Each beam can shine out to three thousand feet."

"What're they, carbon arc?"

"No. Carbon arc puts out more power, but you have to shut down the beam ten minutes every hour to replace the carbon rods. Those are quartz crystal beams with halon lamps. The man who operates it told me the motor that powers the whole assembly uses two gallons of diesel an hour."

"Pretty good investment for only two gallons an hour. Does it belong to the military?"

"No, this guy was some commercial operator who got caught up in the rescue operation, then threw in his lot with the National Guard."

Stack shook his head and laughed. "What a crazy thing war is. You get the strangest collection of people with the weirdest backgrounds shoved into one place." He looked at Bushnell for a moment. "You know, if not for the war

you and I would have passed each other on the street in
broad daylight and neither of us would have given the
other a second look or thought.''

Bushnell nodded in agreement, then they fell silent.
Stack listened to the other man breathing. He sounded
nervous. They were going into the jaws of hell and Bushnell didn't relish fighting for the turf he and his people
occupied. The world was filled with such souls. Too many
of them. They ran and ran. But in the end they had to face
the world and face it with courage—or die!

One of the Harley-Davidson riders following along
behind the van was Octavio Bonalilla, a man of medium
height and graying, frizzled, short, black hair, a deeply
tanned, lined face, worried gray eyes, and strong forearms
which gave him the muscular grip needed to lock onto
someone and take them down in a fight.

He was also the only Hispanic in the group. A man who
all his life had felt himself to be something other than what
he was, different from how he looked on the outside.
Different somehow from the cultural heritage he had
been born into. A Hispanic who internally was really a
Norte. Just like some black man who identified with the
majority white culture more than his own. His was the
dilemma of every minority surrounded by an overwhelming majority which day and night bombarded him
with its cultural messages.

All his life Bonalilla had attempted to be something else,
denying and downplaying his own Hispanic roots.
Admiring and lusting after the North European even to the
point of wooing and winning a blonde Wasp, marrying
her, and befriending those of the majority culture. Yet
even this did not help. Nor could it obliterate what he was,
where he had come from, and how he looked. Something
he remembered each time he passed a Hispanic on the
street, or dealt with his parents, brothers, sisters, and
relatives from whom he could not divorce himself.

And the world of the Norte, about which he had
fantasized so much, proved, once he was past the barriers,

the same as his in terms of problems, though with a different flavor. The women were like the women he had known in his youth. And when he had fights with his blonde angel, her mouth could be as vicious, as biting, as sarcastic, as hot and hellish as that of any Hispanic princess he had fought with. What made it worse was when she called him a dirty, greasy, slimy, little Spic. Something he would not have been called by a Hispanic woman from his own background. and though she later apologized and said she was sorry, the hurt still remained—as well as the question about whether, in the depths of her soul, this was what she really thought of him. He had given up so much to be a part of their world, but sensed that in their heart of hearts, though they accepted him on the surface, he was only an outsider, tolerated to a degree, a better specimen of the lowly Spic class. Their token Hispanic. Their pet Spic.

And now that he'd had a taste of their world, perhaps with the wisdom that comes with age and experience, he'd come to realize that no man could outrun his roots. That in the end you had to be what you were. Bonalilla grew disillusioned with the Nortes and their world. Not that it was a bad place. But it was a world for them, reflecting their tastes, their roots, not his. And while it was nice to occasionally experience what others were doing and had done in their cultures, a man shouldn't have to give up his innards for it. With the passage of time, to his surprise, Bonalilla grew tired of their Norte ways and women and longed for the girls of his youth and the world of his parents. Sadly, his parents were no longer around. He had never given them the happiness they deserved, or spent the time with them that they merited before they passed into the grave. In the twilight of their days they had known what he had done and how ashamed he was of them and their kind as he sold out to the other world. How he wished at that moment to tell them he had come full circle. And that one of the reasons he stayed with these bikers was that they would help him find the survivors of his culture. The remnants of his roots. And not the blonde Norte woman he had divorced and who was now a deep, sharp, bitter scar on the periphery of his consciousness.

As they went past where the bikers had set up their open-air grill, Bonalilla was pulled from his thoughts of yesterday into the greater horror of today, remembering that they hadn't eaten yet and were still hungry. But that didn't matter so much now. More important events had intruded.

They took a sidestreet to the right. Another place full of rubble. They all looked the same after a while. A few more minutes passed this way before the van stopped slowly in a cloud of concrete dust.

They got off their bikes as Stack and Bushnell came out of the van. Stack told them to take the weapons and ammunition from the van in case there was an attack.

Bushnell, now in his element, took the lead and everyone followed as he led them through a gap in a 20-foot-high wall and over piles of rubble into the guts of what had once been a building but now lay open to the sky. Stack saw cars under mountains of rubble, and figured that perhaps this had been some sort of garage. If they could be dug out, some of the vehicles might still be useable or good sources of spare parts.

Bushnell, looking back to see if they were following, led them through holes in other walls, down a debris-filled alley, over fallen doors, through open doorways, then down stairs into a cellar. There, standing at an open doorway, in shadow, was a woman with a club.

"It's me," Bushnell said in a loud whisper. "I've got friends with me. People who'll protect us."

"Wait," she said, sudden excitement in her voice. Bushnell held up his hand for them to wait. They stood there, listening to her clambering over rubble, chunks of stone or brick falling down with clicking sounds. After several minutes and distant talking three people came back toward them. The woman with the club and a man and woman.

The man looked in his late 40s with messy grayish-black

hair. He was wearing rimless glasses. The woman with him was in her middle 20s, her brown hair done up in a loose bun. They looked like aging hippies. The man introduced himself as William Galoris and the woman told them her name was Joy Church. She had a wide, round, friendly face and innocent-seeming eyes still amazed by the wonder of life. But in that look something new had appeared: a horror that a war such as this could happen to mankind in general and them in particular. The person with them, the woman with the club, was in her 40s, with long, straggly, unwashed hair, and introduced herself as Janet Kagle.

Stack introduced a few of the people on his side, then asked to see their quarters and how many of them there were. Galoris nodded and with a slight smile led the way.

They passed through another cellar, part of which was open to the sky, then down stairs through an opening in the opposite wall to a cellar lower down. This one was dark, with a small fire in one corner which gave heat and light. A dull, flickering orange glow which barely brushed away the shadows, only to have them return the next second. Stack could see the grayish gleam of teeth and eyes as people looked their way. It was impossible to tell age or sex in the darkness. But gradually, as they stood there, the visitors grew used to the blackness.

The floor they walked across had large cracks in it and the ceiling was overgrown with piping. "Part of our people are here," Galoris told them. "Now I'll show you where the rest are." They followed him, listening to his voice, which sounded different in the enclosed stygian moistness. He took them into a room half filled with sacks containing produce.

"Potatoes," he announced. "A plentiful if monotonous diet."

Stack wanted to tell Galoris about the meat they'd brought and to joke that now they could have steak and french fries. But he didn't know Galoris well enough to make jokes, not wanting to look foolish or insensitive.

Galoris next took them through a large hole in the wall

to their right. They entered a wide concrete tunnel with people around a fire inside. A hundred feet down on their left was another fire with more people around it. Stack surmised the wall between the cellar and tunnel had been knocked down by the shock effect of the nuclear bombs going off.

The ten-foot-wide tube they stood inside of stretched endlessly away to the right and left into darkness where the fires could no longer thrust away the shadows anymore.

No one had to tell the visitors what this was. They were inside a sewer tube that had been drained in the convulsion following the war, and those who had taken shelter here had found this breech into the sewer.

The visitors felt the cool breeze which wafted across their faces as they smelled the slightly sour sewer smell and the distant sea from somewhere far off and listened to the sounds people around fires make, which sounded unearthly in this place.

Galoris let them look a moment longer, then said, "What you've seen is our new home. Pretty, ain't it?"

"How many of you are there?" Courtner wanted to know.

"Thirty-one, including fifteen children under age sixteen. Nine of our people died in the bombings and a few were injured. Not badly. Thank God they're still mobile. We're also damned lucky to have found this place. One of the cellars here must've belonged to a produce company. For that reason we have potatoes to eat and some cabbage also. You're all free to join us while our larder lasts."

"Thank you, no," Courtner said. "We have provisions. All we need is a place to cook our food."

"We can help you gather wood," Joy Church offered.

"No need. We'll gather the wood. We don't want to be a burden."

"You're not," Galoris said.

"Any rats here?" Stack asked.

"Some," Joy Church told him. "But they're no problem."

"They won't be while they have dead flesh to eat," Stack said. "But that won't last. Then those buggers will be looking for your food. You'd better put out a day and night guard to watch the kids. Rats aren't shy about what they'll eat. We had a nice little run-in with them while coming to San Francisco." He looked at the bikers and they smiled back uneasily.

"Okay," Courtner said. "Now that we've had the grand tour, I'd like for my people to have lunch, which has been sadly delayed. While we eat you can fill us in more specifically about the people causing this trouble and where they can be found. We'll then figure out a plan to stop them dead. Or maybe we can meet face to face and have a peace powwow. The last thing Americans should be doing after the start of a nightmare like this is fighting one another." He got a chorus of agreement. But saying it here and convincing others elsewhere were two different things.

The men were taken back upstairs, where they had left the guns and ammo, then some of the bikers went to get their food from the van while Galoris got them pots and pans, bent and battered, but still good for cooking. He offered them potatoes for a stew. Stack provided spices and seasonings left over from his camping trip. Soon, the cellar was full of good cooking smells. More wood was gathered and thrown on the fire, which crackled warmly, creating a false, bright cheer, sparks flying up from it and dying in the blackness above the orange glow of flames spreading a half circle of light across the room and the surrounding walls, interrupted by occasional sputterings, sizzling, and long, gray plumes of smoke as the food cooked and bubbled.

Courtner realized they would't be able to avoid sharing the meat with the people here, even though this meant cutting back on their provisions, in order to create a better bonding and deeper cooperation so that the two groups might operate as smoothly and efficiently as possible to quickly triumph over the adversaries they both faced. And the sooner this problem was solved, the sooner the visitors could get on with the task they had set themselves.

"I'll bet your people haven't had meat in days," Courtner suggested to Galoris with a wide smile and a sly glance at Stack. "Why don't you join us? Potatoes alone can't be satisfying, even with cabbage."

"Thank you kindly, but not not everyone here eats meat. Many were vegetarians before the war."

"Yes, but right now they need all the nutrition they can get to survive what'll be coming down the road. And no one can say what that'll be. Has any radiation sickness hit here yet?"

"We got it the day after the bombings and almost lost two people. But most of us have recovered, except for some kids who still suffer chills and diarrhea."

"The same happened in the mountains. If there are no new infusions of radiation-laden dust in the air, that might be the last of the radiation we'll see for a while. Of course, I can't tell what the effects will be from ingesting radiation-laden food and water. But that can't be helped. People need to eat and drink. By the way, where do you get your water?"

"From several small lakes and reservoirs inside the city," Joy Church broke in and explained. "They're full of debris, but we boil the water, which we bring back in bottles and buckets. To the northwest there's College Hill Reservoir bordering on Holly Park. To the southeast is University Mount Reservoir, which is actually two bodies of water separated by Bacon Street."

"It's good that you have no freshwater worries for awhile. But right now you'd better call together your vegetarians and tell them this may be their last chance in a long time to have a beef supper."

Galoris did so. But he didn't have to spend much time convincing them. A good jolt will change people's habits and beliefs to a significant degree. It wouldn't be the first time that had happened, Stack thought. Then he sent one of the bikers to bring more meat. Galoris, meanwhile, came back with people from the sub-cellar and sewer tunnel.

They were a grinning, motley lot, made more so by the bombing. They looked to Stack like a bunch of cavemen and cave women dressed up in the clothing of today. For one second he even expected them to begin grunting instead of talking. But talk they did and in fairly good English too. The illusion quickly died.

Extra pots were soon brought out for the added meat and potatoes. More wood was put on the fire, making it hotter and wider as pots were set out to cook on circular stands of gathered brick.

Bushnell stepped over to Stack. "Thanks for the meat, but that doesn't solve our problem. After this meal is eaten and digested, the dilemma will still be with us."

"We haven't forgotten what the problem is and intend to take care of it. But we can't do it alone. People in your group are going to have to volunteer to carry the fight to the enemy."

Listening to this, Galoris and Joy Church came over. Galoris touched his chest. "We're a peaceful people, sir. Not warlike. If the world were made up of folks like us there would never have been a Third World War."

"But the world isn't made up of people like you. There are Soviets, Cubans, North Vietnamese, Iranians, and Libyans out there. It's a tough place, mister."

"I understand. But we're not part of it. Look around, sir. What do you see? Men, women, and children. Peaceful people. The older ones among us are former hippies, graduates of Haight-Ashbury, remnants of the Age of Aquarius, the anti-war movement, the anti-nuclear movement. This is not our way."

"Are you finished?"

Galoris nodded.

"Good. You've said your piece. Now I'm going to say mine." Stack looked from face to face. The faces of the men who'd come with him and the faces of the people who lived here.

He touched his chest and let his hand drop. "I'm old enough to remember the hippies, the anti-war movement, all of it. I was never a hippie. I never marched against the war. I believed the Vietnam War was right then and I believe the same thing now. I've always believed in a strong military and, though I don't know what caused this war, I sincerely believe that had we been stronger we'd still be at peace now. But this isn't the time to argue about Vietnam, the sixties, or how well prepared we were militarily. None of that has anything to do with what we face now. The issue here is whether you want to live or die. Are your asses worth protecting? You have three choices. Run, stay and fight, or stay and die. Whether you run or not doesn't matter. Those bastards out there," he pointed toward the outside world, "will just pick someone else to shoot down. They've got to be stopped. Now will you help, or shirk your responsibilities?"

"We're not fighters," Galoris repeated.

"Fine, you're lovers," Stack said sarcastically. "But there's a time to make love and a time to kick ass. Till now you could depend on your country to protect you. You could depend on someone else to do the fighting while you watched TV and ate bonbons, or whatever it is you did before the bombs began to drop. However, we're now in a post-nuclear world. A place where you must do your own battling. Actions, not words, talk loudest here. You can run, you can give up, you can slink away with your tails between your legs. But down the next road, around the next bend, you'll run into some other mob which wants this, that, or the other, and you'll either have to give it up or die. Or you can try running. But maybe they'll be faster and you won't make it. Suppose they ask for your women so they can have a harem? Suppose they want your kids so they can have cheap child labor in their fields? Will you give them up? Where will it end?"

Stack fell silent and watched their faces. This was reality speaking. A reality they couldn't escape. Bushnell didn't wait for Galoris. He stepped forward.

"I'm with you. I'm tired of being fucked. I don't know how to fight. But if you're willing to teach me, I'm willing to learn."

"I'm glad you've come over. How about the rest of you?" He looked at Galoris whose face was filled with tension and indecision, but did not expect anything.

"Well, I'll let you think it over while we eat. But then we're going to have to have your answers. Since we don't have the strength of the enemy we'll need every man . . . and every woman who can hold a gun." His eyes swept their faces. No one answered.

"I'll also need information from anyone who can give it about the enemy. Anything and everything from how they look to where they're located. If this must end in gunplay, I don't want us going in blind. So I'm going to make a soft probe of where they're at to have a look-see at what's happening."

A mousy-haired girl, with thick glasses like the bottom of soda-pop bottles that distorted her eyes, stepped forward and began to tell about the enemy encampment 20 rubble-filled blocks away, giving him street names and cross streets. Stack held up a hand.

"Street signs don't mean shit. There are no street signs to speak of and no streets in many places. The landscape's been altered. One or two of you may have to come along to show me this place."

"I'll go," Bushnell quickly volunteered.

"Good. Now how many of them are there?"

"Dozens," one voice said. Others agreed.

"How many dozens?"

"No one knows," Bushnell said. "We've been running and hiding, not stopping and counting."

"Why hide here?" Courtner asked. "Why not farther away?"

"This is as good a place as any," Galoris answered. "And they don't know we're here. There's room enough in this place for everyone, which we might not have elsewhere, and a sewer to run and hide in if someone comes. Even if we went two or three miles away, don't you think they'd be able to find us there too? They can walk that distance."

"How long have you been hunted?" Angelicus asked.

"About a day and a half."

"Maybe they'll stop."

"That kind doesn't stop unless they're stopped," Stack interjected.

"Perhaps you can reason with them," Galoris suggested.

"Have you tried?" Courtner wanted to know.

"Yes, but all we got for our troubles was shot at. So we vacated the place where we were and found this place. Will you try and reason with them?"

"Maybe. We'll see how things go down. It's difficult to decide in advance how something should go." He looked at Stack. "Right?" The other man smiled back. Both had learned how strange, hard, and contrary life could be. Not that they didn't know this before the war. Only, now it had been brought home to them harder and harsher than before.

"Who else besides gays and yourselves are these people going after?" Stack wanted to know.

"Russians," Galoris said. Stack's face was cracked by lines of curiosity. "There are rumors," Galoris continued, "about the Soviets landing commandos along the coast by submarine. Any Russians, or suspected Soviets, all immigrants, are in danger."

"I see," Stack said, shaking his head. Then he asked, "How can they tell who's gay and who isn't?"

"They can't. But if this person or that looks gay, that's enough for them. And the fear of AIDS makes it worse. According to them, from what they've been screaming at us, gays will pollute the water and spread AIDS even faster now that everyone's resistance has been lowered since the attack due to the bombing and radiation. And we're not the only ones hiding out. There's a gay group nearby, which we met while going for water, headed by a guy named Francis Pelf. They're also lying low. And we've come into contact with Russian immigrants who moved here from the Soviet Union to find a new life. Since they look Russian, or speak English with a Russian accent, they're in prime danger.''

"Perfect,'' Courtner commented. "It's not bad enough that we have to face radiation and all the other hells this war has brought down, but we have fanaticism and the worst sort of lies and rumors to make us fight among ourselves and hunt down fellow Americans. What a bitch life's turned out to be.'' Disgust was written all over his face.

At this point one of the women doing the cooking announced that the first of the food was ready. Bowls, cracked dishes, metal pots and pans of every description appeared, also spoons, knives, and bent pieces of metal good for scooping food up, many of these utensils having been partly bent or melted by the blast and heat.

As food was ladled out the cellar filled with the pungent aroma of meat, cooked potatoes, and cabbages, spices, and seasonings. For the moment hunger took over and people forgot the war and their troubles as they hungrily swallowed down, sometimes with only a little chewing, pieces of savory meat and hot potatoes, even burning their mouths. That didn't matter as long as the food could be shoveled in and swallowed down as fast as possible.

Stack was surprised at how hungry he was and how this intruded on his thoughts, almost blocking out all other sensations, speculations, and wonder. Galoris, on the other hand, did not let his hunger get the better of him. Midway through his meal he looked around at the heads bent over plates, mugs, and pans, almost like members of some great tribe sitting in their cave, around a fire, eating the evening's hunting catch. And he was the great tribal chief. Funny. He didn't feel like a chief.

Someone tapped him on the shoulder. He'd been so deep in thought he hadn't even noticed Stack walk up.

"Bushnell's leaving with me for our soft probe. When I get back I'll be able to tell you about the enemy strength and lineup.''

"How long will it take?''

"An hour and a half, maybe longer. One can't tell. There are always complications."

"I see. Okay. Good luck," Galoris said absentmindedly, as if he'd been taken from a place better than this and wanted to return to a world now gone.

He began to eat again as Stack told Courtner, "Put three or four guys on night perimeter patrol in case these monkeys find out where we are and decide to pay us a visit."

"Right," Courtner answered, his eyes seemingly confused as if he too had been marching across the Great Plains of his mind.

Stack walked over to Bushnell. "Finished eating?" Bushnell nodded and put his bowl down, his face suddenly drawn. As they headed from the cellar one of the nearer women smiled at Stack and said, "Good luck."

"Thanks, we'll need it." Then they headed outside into the dying light of day.

6

"You are a Syrian Lion," Mohammed Yahzdi said with a wide, yellow, toothy smile as he looked at Ismail Salamis Farouky, his main lieutenant. Farouky, a man with a long, narrow face, dark brown fanatic's eyes, a bulging forehead, and overhanging Neanderthal brows, grinned at this praise. He was a Syrian Arab who'd been in the U.S. over eight years and before the war had worked in the local fish-packing industry.

Yahzdi, a former Iranian student who had demonstrated for years against the Shah, had returned to Iran to enjoy the glorious regime of Ayatollah Ruhollah Khomeini, and wound up fighting for five years against Iraq before he deserted and made his way back to America as a refugee. Ever since he had worked in book stores for various radical-front Islamic and Arab groups. Though he had fled Iran, enough of the fiendish mind disease of fanaticism had rubbed off to radicalize his reactions to almost everything. Now, in this place and time, he had become the leader he had always wanted to be. Yahzdi was no longer young. But he came from a place in the world where one could be a murderous pimp in old age. A pimp who kills, crushes, and destroys, then expects heaven at the end of it all.

Yahzdi, at this point in life, had iron gray hair, a short blackish-gray beard, hard eyes, a short, wide-pored nose, thick, unsmiling lips, and dark skin burned to a fine tan by

the hot California sun, as it had once been tanned by the
Mideastern sun of his native Iran when he'd worked for his
uncle chopping wood in the forests of the Elbruz
Mountains. He'd also worked two summers fishing for
sturgeon in the Caspian Sea to the north. There he'd met a
young girl whom he'd later raped. In the Shah's Iran that
meant prison. In the Iran of Khomeini it might have meant
death. Yahzdi had fled to Turkey. Then, having purchased
false papers, he'd come first to England, then to America,
where he'd worked various jobs before starting night
school, hoping to earn a degree in economics.

America was a freer land than Iran or any Moslem
nation. He'd lost many of the inhibitions he had grown up
with in the strict society of his youth. Though afraid of this
freedom, he'd felt better about himself than he'd felt at
home. He'd discovered, though he could not put
it into words, what a harsh, oppressive thing religion
could be when it came to sex. And this was true not
only of Islam, but many other religions as well. However, eventually his inner instincts, the things he had
learned as a youth, augmented by the strain and nightmare
of Khomeini-ism, had come to the fore. And now he was
back in America, carrying out in miscrocosm some of the
sick things he had learned in Iran. And there were enough
people in his mixed Arab, Iranian, and American group
for him to hold sway over a fairly large area.

Bigotry, a sedentary disease born in dark minds in dim
rooms, had come into the open. These two men, standing
by a broken wall inside their stronghold, were con-
gratulating themselves on work well done. Two hundred
yards away, standing on the second floor of a ruined
building, looking out through a broken window, two men
witnessed the pair by the wall.

"We're going closer," Stack whispered to Bushnell.
"Answer me quietly, sound travels farther than you
think." Bushnell nodded. Stack then said, "I wonder who
those two guys are."

"We'll find out eventually," Bushnell answered,

perhaps a bit too loud. Stack did not reply as he led the way down to the ground atop the rubble of what had once been the inner contents of this six-story apartment building with a shell still standing.

Stack worked his way carefully down. He had an M-16 rifle in one hand and wore his hunting knife belt with four sheathed knives hanging from it. Bushnell had an M-16 rifle which he had never used. The only rifles he had fired had been at carnivals for kewpie dolls. And he never won any.

Once on the ground they began to make their way forward. About 50 yards from the enemy base Stack whispered. "We'll wait behind this wall," he pointed to it, "till total darkness falls. The night hides many things. I'll go forward alone and do the scouting and you wait here till I come back."

"How will you know how to get back? Everything looks the same."

"This wall is next to the street. I'll just move along the road, looking for certain landmarks as I make my way forward to where the enemy is. Coming back, I'll follow the same path. And should this take longer than expected, don't worry, just be patient and wait. Do not come forward to try and find me. You may fall into someone's trap." He paused. "And if I don't come back in two hours, leave. That means I've been caught or killed."

Bushnell looked grimmer, but Stack smiled. "Cheer up. The future's ours." With that, he slipped into the gathering darkness now creeping across the devastated land with a blanket for troubled sleepers.

Stack made his way slowly forward, eyeing every dip, fold, and rubble heap for hidden sentries, but saw no one. Then, as he got closer to where the two men had stood—the spot was now empty—he spotted a reddish glow behind a group of battered walls. Fires. Either for cooking, light, or heat. Stack moved faster now, though he urged himself to slow down and watch the landscape. Lack of caution had cost many men their heads, and he vowed his would not be added to the total.

Trying to move as soundlessly as possible so as not to set off any rubble slides, he approached what had once been the wall of a building and which now consisted of varying heights depending on how hard the blast had hit each portion. He came to a lower section of the wall and looked over at a long, open area which consisted of walls that had once partitioned rooms in a much larger building whose upper floors had been sheared off. Now, behind some walls Stack could see men moving between rooms amid sounds of talking and laughter.

But he could not tell how many men there were. Stack decided to circle the ruin, which he guessed had once been a factory or a warehouse. By looking in from every angle he might see all there was to be seen. As he circled, Stack looked for hidden sentries, but found none. These people were either inexperienced, or felt damned safe.

Stack had become almost another man as he carried out his self-appointed mission. His face had turned hard, the skin drawn tight over the bones, his eyes slitted, endlessly alert, his nostrils flaring, his mouth mean and twisted, his hands squeezing harder on his rifle, his ears alert, almost raised, like the ears of a cat on the stalk. And in this manner he moved slowly along the outside wall of the enemy position, his head pivoting this way and that, his eyes glancing through every gap. He saw parts of bodies, or bodies in pairs, but always in shadow or silhouette.

Stack knew he would have to go inside, but not till he finished circling the perimeter, and that took almost 15 minutes. The night had grown darker in that time, and the glow of the fire within the gates brighter, and the talk of the men inside the walls louder and cheerier.

When Stack had seen everything on the outside, he knew it was time to go in. He also knew that if he were caught, surrounded and outnumbered, the end would not be pretty. But Stack was a man who took chances. He found a gap, entered, then went left down a dark passage without a roof. Doorways and rooms without ceilings opened to either side. A glow came from one of the rooms halfway down on the right. Stack moved toward it, looking back to make sure no one was following along behind. He quickly entered the room and shifted to the right with his back against the wall and waited, breathing heavily, letting his eyes get used to the room, his ears alert like sensors as he listened for the sounds of some approaching enemy.

The reason there was a glow coming from this place was because of a ceiling-to-floor crack in the wall opposite the doorway from perhaps another room. Stack advanced toward the brightness and looked out at another hall, which led to a glowing room full of men who seemed to be eating, drinking, and jesting. Seemed like a nice party. For one moment Stack felt like joining them.

He moved back, standing there in the semi-darkness, wondering if he could get through the wide crack into the other passage. He could squeeze through, but people might come into the hall and see him, perhaps jammed into the crack, not able to move swiftly one way or the other. And then he would die very quickly. No, that was not the way to go.

He moved out of the room, looking both ways, then headed up the hall to see where it led. He felt like a rat in a maze, not knowing what was around the next corner. But he went on, traveling on sheer guts, realizing that being a forward scout in almost any army was one of the most dangerous, lonely, and ruthless jobs. Hard on the nerves and hard on the flesh if caught. But there were men who did such work, and there always would be as long as there were people on the earth.

Just ahead was a passage branching off to the right. It was partly illuminated and led to the hallway he had looked out on. But now he had to extend his head to look into the hallway. However, he could only look in one direction at a time, not seeing anyone who might be coming up from behind. Stack had no choice and would have to chance it.

He looked out into the hall to his left, saw nothing, then

immediately shifted to his right. Someone was coming, but
hadn't seen him because the light wasn't endlessly bright in
all places and because only half his head and one eye had
been extended very briefly and had almost merged in with
the line of the wall.

Stack pulled back, moving into the deeper darkness to
allow the person in the hall to pass. When he'd gone, Stack
moved forward into the hall and toward the room from
which most of the light and noise was coming. As he
reached it, he looked both ways, then extended half his
head and one eye past the doorpost, doing a quick two-
second eyeball reconnaisance of the room beyond.

A roaring fire was going in the middle of the room. A
fire with dozens of men around it. Arabs and Arab-
looking individuals who might or might not be Iranians.
Mixed in with them were Americans. And all of them
were armed with guns. Hunting rifles and shotguns mostly.
Also pistols and hunting knives. Where had they gotten
them? He didn't know. But that question would be
answered in time.

Stack quickly drew back, moved down the lit hall, back
through the side hall, and into the passage he had used to
enter the labyrinth. He moved a bit more swiftly now, his
breathing perhaps too deep, his heart beating too fast with
excitement and with fear. He would be glad to be away
from this place. There was danger in the maze. A danger so
strong it hung on the air and seeped into the very bones of
any outsider who entered it.

Stack reached the end of the passage and began to move
out of the ruins, leaving via the same gap he had used to
get in, when he stopped. With his peripheral vision he
caught sight of something off to the far right. Stack pulled
back, then peeked out and saw a single man in the darkness. At first he looked like a sentry with his back to the
ruins and his eyes peering anxiously into the debris of the
perimeter he had been ordered to guard. But then it
became apparent he wasn't guarding anything. His hands
were at crotch level.

Stack grinned. This guy had just gone out to take a leak. With that realization, Stack moved out quickly from his place of concealment, putting his rifle against the wall as he tried to advance soundlessly toward his victim, making sure at the same time that no one was sneaking up on him. A lot of guys, moving in for the kill, forget they too can be stalked. Stack didn't as he made his lightning strike, one of his hunting knives out as an arm snaked around the man's neck and pulled back at the same time that the knife came around under the man's throat, the point of it digging into the soft flesh just below the chin.

Pushing hard enough to hurt without puncturing the skin and drawing blood, Stack said, in a loud, breathless whisper, "One sound, one cry, and you're heaven's meat."

"Don't stab, mister, don't stab," a hard, tight, scared voice gasped.

"Good. Just don't do anything stupid and you might live out this night and a lot of days and nights to come."

"Sure, sure. Whatever you say."

He could feel the tension in the man's muscles and listened as air wheezed in and out of lungs grasped by fear. The full extent of his power over life was stunning. Stack felt almost godlike and didn't like it. Death this close was too uncomfortable. Stack was no cold-blooded killer. At least not yet. But he would take life if he had to.

"Just walk. I'm holding onto you." The man began to say something. "Don't talk. Just do it." Stack looked left-right, hoping no one else had appeared in the meantime.

The man began to move and Stack headed him behind two rubble mounds on the left. "Okay, stop."

"Don't kill me. Please don't kill me."

"I won't if I get what I want."

"I haven't much money. A watch, two rings. That's all," he gasped.

"I don't want your watch, your rings, or your money."

"You ain't a queer, are you?" the man asked, suddenly afraid that he might be raped.

"I'm not gay, I just want information. How many of you are there?"

"Forty-five, maybe fifty."

"And you're out to kill all gays?"

"Yeah. They're spreadin' AIDS."

"You have that on good medical authority?" Stack asked sarcastically.

"They're doin' it. Honest, man, they are."

Stack saw he was talking to a fool, and didn't bother to explain AIDS was mostly passed through sex and needles and that straights were spreading it too. Instead, he asked, "What's your name?"

"Steven Palermos."

"How'd you come to join this group and how'd the others join up?"

"It just happened. Word spread, people joined. I was on what was left of the waterfront, the place where I used to work, when some of my surviving friends came around, told me what was going down, and asked if I'd join, I said yes and here I am. If we can finish off the queers there won't be no AIDS epidemic. And that'll make it easier for the rest of us to survive."

"It's wrong, mister. You can't go around doing that to other Americans. And even if your idea of stopping AIDS worked, how can you prevent yourself from killing innocent people by mistake?"

"That always happens in war," Palermos said. "Look at all the civilians who get killed when two armies fight in a city."

"Well, that won't be allowed to happen here. I'm going to let you go, buddy. I want you to tell your people that a defense force is being formed to stop them. But we won't go to war unless we have to. I'm willing to negotiate an agreement with your leader under a flag of truce. Let him give us a signal tomorrow night by firing ten times in the air from a single rifle. I'll then come to him under a flag of truce. Got that?"

"Yeah, yeah," the other man answered, eager to be

away from there. Stack turned him around and was about to let him go when he remembered the rifle he had left behind and walked Palermos toward that spot. He let go of his prisoner with one hand, while still keeping the knife in place, grabbed the rifle, pulled the knife away, moved back, and pointed the weapon at Palermos.

"Stay, just stay," Stack said as he backed away. When he reached the rubble mounds, he said, "Go, you're free," then turned and hurried away, not even waiting to see the other man flee. Palermos ran and yelled for help at the same time.

Stack headed for the road, but banged into bricks and hit a wall in the darkness. Still, his eyes had pretty much gotten used to the blackness and he was able to move along, amid the obstacles, with a fair amount of speed and was soon back at the wall behind which Bushnell waited.

"What happened?" Bushnell wanted to know as the night exploded with running and shouting back where Palermos had been released.

"Let's get the hell outta here. They're looking for me. I'll explain it all as we go along. You lead. You know the way."

Bushnell, the pounding of his heart making it feel as if it were coming out of his chest, was confused about direction as they headed through gaps in walls, over debris, across piles of broken, singed lumber and protruding lengths of metal tubing and rods like deadly spears in some African thorn field. Bushnell wanted to stop and reorient himself, but didn't dare. Those bastards sounded very close. Luckily, the night served as a sheltering cloak. Stack watched the moving back of his guide as he followed it up, over, and around obstacles, the tension sweat of the escape filling him with heat, running out now through every pore of his glistening skin, down through his hair and across his moist palms, from which the gun he carried threatened to slip.

Sights and sounds were magnified and seemed to fly past the ears and eyes like swift, lined images watched from a racing train, barely registering on the senses before a new set of images took their place. Stack huffed and puffed, feeling a bit out of breath as he rushed after Bushnell, but not daring to stop or slow down. Nor did he have time, between gasps, to tell Bushnell what had happened.

About 100 yards back Yahzdi and his men fanned out over a 100-yard wide front and advanced like beaters in the bush driving elephants or tigers toward the waiting hunters. But the night, the head start their quarry had achieved, and the vastness of the rubble fields made for too many places to search through, too many places to hide in, too many directions in which their enemies could have gone.

"Bastards," Yahzdi thought, his eyes burning bright, his nostrils flaring, his mouth an open maw like a hunting shark's. He'd kill them, break them open, show them what he was made of. How dare they try and reason with him? Those bastards wouldn't escape their destiny no matter what.

But Stack and Bushnell made their escape. As they got farther away, increasing the distance between themselves and their hunters, the two men slowed down, and Bushnell asked if they could stop to rest.

"Sure, but not for long. The sooner we get back to where we started, the better.

"What happened?" Bushnell asked, his face a pale blur in the greater blackness of night.

"I scouted out their HQ, then grabbed a guy who'd gone out to take a leak. He told me about the fifty bastards in their group. A mixed band of Iranians, Arabs, and Americans. People with a strong dose of homophobia and an unreal fear of AIDS who think the cure for this problem is wiping out all gays. And they couldn't care less if they destroy a lot of others in the process. I wanted to meet the head guy for a powwow tomorrow. But the reception they just gave us is their answer. If these bastards aren't stopped they'll kill your people, any gays they come across, the Russians, and a lot of innocents in between. Now let's get going."

Bushnell nodded, then led the way. In 20 minutes they entered the cellars as Galoris and Courtner, expectant looks on their faces, came forward. Stack quickly dashed any hopes they might have had. When he had finished talking, Galoris's face hardened. He now knew what had to be done.

"I've been thinking over what you told me earlier," he said to Stack. "All my life I've lived one way. I never imagined another path could be right. But after what those animals have done, I must conclude there's no choice but to fight. I want you to train us in how to use the guns you brought along so we can clear these animals from the city and then be able to live some sort of life, no matter how hard and treacherous."

"I'm glad that's your decision. I was worried about how you'd meet this challenge. I would've hated to go out against the numbers they've got with only our small force. What we need now is to meet with the other people attacked by these bandits to get recruits from them."

"When do you want to meet these groups?" Galoris asked.

"Now."

"Okay, I'll take you there."

"I'm going too," Courtner said.

"And while we're gone," Stack suggested, "the guard should be doubled in case those darlings find this place."

"They don't know where we are yet," Galoris stated.

"Right, but they might come across the bunker by accident. While our people stand guard everyone else should stay inside ready to hide in the sewer tunnel if need be."

"Perhaps we shouldn't leave at a time like this," Galoris countered.

"They might or might not come," Stack replied. "Or they could come tomorrow. But we can't wait. We must act now. The sooner these animals are stopped, the better. Come," he said to both men as they followed him out to the van.

"Where to first?" Stack asked Galoris.

"South to see Francis Pelf, head of the surviving West Coast Gay Alliance. At least half a dozen of his people have been snuffed so far. Then we'll go see the Russians. They too have gathered in one place. I also believe some of them are armed."

"Even better. Our supply of guns isn't endless," Stack said.

With that, they moved out, not using headlights at first so as not to give away the location of their hiding place. Stack drove slowly and carefully, even after he put on the headlights. Here and there, all around, like stars in the night, firelights glowed till hundreds undulated across the ruined city. Survivors seeking heat, light, and fire to cook their food with. How many had survived inside the city? Twenty thousand? More? Less? He didn't know the answer and doubted anyone else did either. Then he remembered he had forgotten to ask Palermos where the mob had gotten their guns. Stack silently chided himself for being so forgetful.

The minutes passed quickly as they made their way through the urban desert. Stack suddenly felt very tired and looked at himself in the rearview mirror. He didn't like what he saw and his thoughts were not any better. He seemed to himself, in that moment, to be nothing more than a small bump on a giant log. A man stripped of all humanity, all connections, every bit of importance by a cruel horror he hadn't asked for or expected. He wanted to curse somebody. But who? The people who fired the bombs which struck this place? Yes. The evil leaders who gave the orders? Definitely. But his curses ran deeper and wider. He cursed those lawmakers who had cut our defense budgets to the point where we were made vulnerable. He cursed the people in and out of government who had been against SDI. How many warheads got through which otherwise wouldn't have made it? Stack hated them all with an intense fury and sincerely hoped none of them had survived the first fires of conflagration even as their victims did not.

Feeling more bitter then at anytime since the war began, Stack went where Galoris instructed, only half his mind on the road ahead. It seemed that they drove for about 20 minutes before Galoris said stop and they got out.

Galoris then led them into ruins with flickering lights showing through in places. As he came to an open doorway leading down into a cellar, he shouted out, "Peace, peace, we come as brothers. Peace."

Two men stepped out. One had short-cropped brown hair. The other had long, reddish hair down to his shoulders. Looking at them, Stack was unable to tell that they were gay. The sight of the armed men with Galoris frightened the two who had come up from inside.

"They're friends, here to help us," Galoris said in order to calm them. Sudden smiles appeared on their faces. "Is Francis here?"

"Sure," the redhead answered. "Follow us."

They went down broken steps into a cellar. The roof had been ripped off for about half its length. The hall seemed to go on forever. Dim illumination came from rooms opening off to both sides. Going past they could see groups of males on cots, or bedding, or sitting atop bundles of clothing and other possessions. Some had tables and chairs probably liberated from dwellings where some furniture had remained intact.

They went left into a room at the end of the corridor. Sitting on a milk box, behind a folding table, writing something, with a mug of coffee steaming on the table, was a young man, with rimless glasses and long, brown hair combed straight back onto his shoulders. He looked around 28. His hair was receding in front and he had a high, wide forehead without lines which made him seem somehow serene. He had big, brown eyes and full, tense lips in an oval face. He was one of those males about whose features one detected something feminine even from a distance.

Pelf nodded to Galoris and said, "So good to see you, Bill. Who're these gentlemen?" The voice sounded slightly feminine, smooth, and modulated. The kind of thing you met in certain gay circles. Stack wondered how Pelf and others like him would operate in the harsh world they had so suddenly been thrust into.

"It's also good to see you," Galoris replied, then added, "The people with me are Nick Stack," he pointed to him, "and Bay Cournter. Two visitors to our fair city." Pelf smiled at the sarcasm. "They've come here about the problem we're all having." Pelf looked at them with more interest. Stack then took over, relating what he had seen and learned and what they needed from Pelf's group.

"How many of your people have ever used guns and are willing to fight?"

Pelf picked up the mug of coffee and drank from it, thinking all the while, his eyes screwed up as he ran through his memory files. As this was happening an obviously gay male in his early 20s with long, dark hair, which had obviously been and still was being well taken care of, walked in, cast some approving looks Stack's way—which made Stack uneasy—then went over to Pelf and in a feminine-sounding voice asked, "Would you like some more coffee?"

"No, thank you," Pelf then pointed to the young man, who looked somewhat like a girl Stack had gone out with in high school, which made Stack a bit more uneasy. "This is Gravy Train. That's what we call her—I mean, him. Gravy Train used to work in the burlesque line at Thunderworks, a major erotic theater here in the city before the war. Gravy Train knows a lot of fellas and would be better able to answer your questions."

Stack then told Gravy Train what he was looking for. Gravy Train put a forefinger under his chin, closed his eyes a moment, and thought. Opening his eyes, he looked admiringly at Stack and said, "We have some really butch guys here. Not too many, though. There were more before the war. Some have joined us since then. And if those bastards out there stop bothering us, we'll be able to make a decent home for ourselves." He said it with a lisp some might find cute, but which grated on Stack.

Finally, Stack said, "Could I meet these guys?"

"Sure, I'll get them," Gravy Train answered, and wiggled out.

Courtner grinned at Stack. "If you don't watch it, you'll be going steady soon." Stack didn't answer, but looked at Pelf, who grinned at the joke.

Gravy Train was soon back with two rather tough-looking guys who just barely seemed gay. One was tall, with a balding head of blonde hair, looked in his mid-30s, and was named Bart Boyd. The other, George Boskert, was short and muscular, with brown hair and a hard, square face. The perfect weightlifter type. Gravy Train pointed first to Boyd. "He used to be in the Marines." Then he pointed at Boskert. "And he used to be in the Army."

"What did you two guys do?" Stack asked, looking first at Boyd.

"I was in Nam. Infantry. M-16-trained, and was honorably discharged with the rank of corporal." Boskert was next. It turned out he had been an M-60 tank mechanic, but knew how to use an M-16 rifle and also an M-14.

"We've got M-16s. I hope you fellas aren't shy about using them."

Boyd, a hate-filled look on his face, said, "Just gimme that rifle and point me at those bastards who flamed my friends. I'll show you what a Marine can do. They'll be sorry they were born."

"The same goes for me," Boskert added in a hard, flat voice. Stack looked into his eyes and knew he'd hate to be the man who had to face down Boskert. Gay or not, these guys were tough and able to handle themselves.

"Glad you people have the spirit. We'll need that in combat." Then Stack looked at Pelf. "How many more like these two do you have?"

"Just the two," Pelf answered with a serene smile. "We have about twenty-five people here, and most of them are good only for combing hair and perhaps making bandages and feeding hot soup to the wounded.''

"I understand," Stack said. "Speaking of food, how's your ration situation?"

"We have enough. We've been sending out scouts to intact and fairly intact houses, going through all the rooms for anything useable. We even found a collapsed supermarket. So much inside was still useable. The meat, rancid by then, was being eaten by rats. But there were canned and boxed goods aplenty, though the rats had started on some of the boxed products. Many of the cans are bent, but can still be opened. Want to see our provisions room?"

Courtner and Stack nodded. Pelf rose, led them into the hall, and to a room halfway down on the right. Pelf pulled a candle from his pocket, lit it with a paper match, and took them inside. Besides boxes of candles, dinner-table candles, religious candles in tall glasses, Sabbath candles, and memorial candles, there were endless cans of tuna and salmon, sardine tins, cans of Campbells and Progresso soup, boxes of macaroni dinners, spaghetti boxes, torn sacks of rice—with some of the rice spilled out—flour sacks, small sacks of sugar, dented coffee cans, tea boxes, jars of spaghetti sauce, cans of tomato paste, bars of soap, candies such as M&Ms, Baby Ruth bars, and after-dinner mints, plastic soda bottles—but no place to refrigerate them, bread and donuts in boxes and plastic wrappers, and cartons of cigarettes.

Pelf, who'd been watching the two men, saw where their eyes wandered. "Would you like to have some cartons of cigarettes? We have more than enough."

"Thanks, you don't know how much we appreciate that," Stack said as he and Courtner eyed the available brands. Marlboro 100s, Falcons, Pall Malls, Kent 100s, Starlings, Carltons, and Benson & Hedges. Grinning, Stack took two cartons of Kents. Courtner took one of Pall Malls and another of Sterlings. Galoris picked up two cartons of Marlboro 100s. He didn't smoke, but many of his people did and, if the factories didn't start up soon, cigarettes would quickly become a rare commodity.

Pelf put out his candle and they returned to his office. As he sat down, Stack saw that the illumination in the room was provided by two large religious candles in glasses on a side table.

Pelf quickly asked, "When can we expect the attack to go in?"

"We could start an hour from now if we used just the people we now have," Courtner explained. "But we don't have the numbers, or know the terrain well enough. We want more people in on this first. Which is why we want to see the Russians, and also train volunteers to use the guns we brought along."

"I wish you could attack now," Pelf said.

"So do we all. But sometimes things don't go the way one wants them to. Anyhow, we've got to be moving. Thanks for the cigarettes."

"Forget it. They didn't cost us a thing," Pelf stated with a smile. His visitors grinned, then left.

Once back in the van, Courtner said, "Nice people. Too bad they've been persecuted. I don't agree with their sexual orientation, but that's no reason to kill them."

"The world doesn't work like that," Galoris answered. "When people are frightened, logic and reason don't count. And AIDS is liquid dynamite. Pelf, nice guy that he is, has AIDS. At least that's what I heard."

"You positive?" Stack asked.

Galoris closed his eyes briefly and nodded up and down. "I heard this on good authority."

"But he doesn't look sick," Stack exclaimed.

"When you first catch it, nothing shows. Your body just throws up a wall of antibodies. They don't work, but that's the first indication that you've been infected. Depending on various factors the virus can take from one to twenty years to kill you. Though, on average, six or seven years after infection the victim develops ARC. AIDS-Related Complex. He or she experiences chills, fevers, swollen glands, and other out-of-sorts feelings. In over half the cases ARC sufferers move onto the AIDS phase—the final, fatal stages of the sickness. Sufferers generally last an average of eighteen months. And that's if they're getting adequate medical care. Come down with it in the present world and you're as fucked as those poor natives in Africa who die with practically no medical care. We're going to see a lot of that here.''

"I heard it was pretty bad in Africa," Stack said.

"I read before the war that one hundred fifty million blacks and Arabs were carrying the virus. And that it was epidemic across all of Central Africa from the Atlantic to the Indian Ocean. Also, that it was moving strongly through Ethiopia, South Africa, Nigeria, and Egypt. There was worry that this was the beginning of a Mid-eastern epidemic. Had the war not broken out they would have been devastated anyway. I just wonder what the bombs did to them. Probably made a bad situation worse, like in the Caribbean. I talked to someone who only months ago went to Haiti on vacation. He quickly came back. Every hospital was jammed with AIDS patients and one doctor told him not to have sex with anyone and get the hell out of Haiti. The situation wasn't much better in most other Caribbean nations.''

"It makes it easier to understand why those bastards are going around killing people in the city," Courtner said.

"But that helps no one and makes matters worse," Stack said. "There's never an excuse for lawlessness.''

"I hate to break this up," Galoris told them, "but discussing the problems of the world changes nothing. It just makes us temporarily feel better. And in the real world, that takes a man no place when it comes to confronting the obstacles that need solving.''

Stack grinned. "When did you turn into a philosopher?''

"All of us will be philosophers before this is over. Hard times make for thinking men and women. And thinking leads to a better world.''

"Not always. Look at the world thinking men have

given us. Life would have been better had we remained apes, or whatever it is our ancestors were. Nature would have gone on endlessly, with a pollution-free environment not knowing highways, crime, or nuclear weapons."

"Ain't progress wonderful," Galoris finally said with a laugh. Then he pointed out the van window. "We'd better get going. The Russians are a few miles from here in the Parkmerced area, south of California State University and just east of Lake Merced."

"Means nothing to me. I've never been there."

"Drive. You'll see how it looks when we get there." On that note they started off. The headlights, as they moved through the darkness, were twin fingers of brightness probing the corridors of night, touching rubble, buckled walls, steel girders sticking out of cracked buildings like protruding ribs coming out of the skins of wounded soldiers. They passed sporadic, ghostly lines of people dressed in rags, making their way through the ruins like travelers in the desert. They would first throw their hands up across their faces against the brightness of the lights, then call out and wave as the van passed. Perhaps they wanted to exchange some warmth with other human beings, or ask for food, a lift, or whatever. But time was of the essence and couldn't be wasted as they headed through the rubble fields of the city, ignoring various stimuli, fighting down the natural inclinations of their insides.

They went past places where bright firelights shone out of the ruins, sometimes with great orange sparks hissing off into the darkness. On occasion human forms were silhouetted against the flames, moving, talking, crying, or laughing. Who could tell? The forms were so close, yet so distant, like Neanderthal men and women around some prehistoric campfire, Stack felt a tragic aloneness at that moment, as if thrust from the present into the deep, dark past. He wondered if the others in the van felt the same way, but did not ask, afraid to allow them into his worry and vulnerability. Alone and in silence, he thought of his wife, Marcy, and his children. Missing them now more than ever. Remembering that all he was doing was so he could get back East and find them. But he forced that from his mind. A man operates best with all his thoughts and objectives in one place, like the concentrated rays of the sun which, when gathered by mirrors, can melt steel.

Stack pulled himself out of the cocoon of his thoughts, lit a cigarette, and spoke to his companions. "You know, those gays are no fools. They found the ruins of a supermarket and looted it of everything useable. You people ought to do the same," he said, looking specifically at Galoris.

"I'll get on it as soon as we return to our base," he answered.

"You can also hunt," Courtner added. "Plenty of birds are still in the air."

"But for how long?" Stack asked. "The wildlife in this country wasn't enough to sustain the settlers when we had ten percent of the people we have today. And we had a lot more animals at that time than we have now."

"I worry about today," Courtner said. "Let tomorrow take care of itself."

"It don't work that way, dude," Stack disagreed. "If you don't worry about tomorrow today, tomorrow may be your last day."

"I still don't see it your way. Radiation might kill us meanwhile. What's the use of planning?"

"Let's hope not everybody thinks like that."

"I don't believe anyone's thinking any single way," Galoris interjected. "They're just trying to survive one day at a time."

In the middle of the conversation they came to a fork in the road. "Go right," Galoris said. Stack did, and went three more blocks before Galoris told him to stop. "This is it."

They got out and Stack locked up. One never knew what kind of prowlers were moving about. Then they headed up a two-story-high rubble hill on their right and stood on top as Galoris scanned the terrain till he spotted the lights from two fires. "I think that's them." He pointed west.

They headed back down, Courtner almost tripping, then across the road to a long block where the buildings had survived better than in most other places, and made their way through passages and gaps in buildings til they came to a courtyard only partly filled with debris. In its center had stood a large tree, now blown down into one of the buildings except for ten feet which stuck up out of the earth, the severed portion a mass of sharp, white splinters.

As they entered the courtyard someone suddenly came out of a hole in the wall directly across the way. He had long, black hair and a large, black beard that made him look like a Mexican. His expression was none too friendly. But then Galoris identified himself and asked, "Is Sergei or Yuri here? I've brought friends." The man smiled.

"Wait, I go get them," the man said in heavily accented English. And then he disappeared back through the gap as Stack wondered how long this would take. But in less than a minute the man was back with two others. One was a redheaded man with a wide, flat face, a big, hooked nose, and stringy hair parted in the middle and combed sideways down his head. The other was shorter, barrel-chested, with a close-cropped brown beard and hair the same color. He had thick, reddish lips that stuck out obscenely through the beard.

The redheaded man came forward first. "Sergei," Galoris said, a little too brightly, stepping forward to take his hand. Then he shook hands with the other man. "How arya, Yuri?" Next, he introduced his companions and said to them, "This is Sergei Yusupov, that's Yuri Raskolnikov." They shook hands, though none of them felt any friendliness toward each other, being filled only with the wary wonder of allied soldiers about to go to war against a common enemy.

Galoris quickly explained why these men were here and what they wanted. The Russians looked at Stack and Courtner with sudden respect. These were men with guns.

Men willing to fight and stop evil. A rarity.

"We will help," Yusupov said. "Two of our people were killed by these people and two more injured. They are now in the hospital in Candlestick Park."

"How many people do you have?" Stack asked.

"Twenty-eight. We are not many. There were seventy of us before the bombs came down. Some lived a while after the explosions, a few of them pinned under fallen buildings. Some died because things fell on them. Others died of burns or radiation poisoning."

"How many can fight?"

"There are sixteen males. A dozen above the age of fifteen. Half of those have had military training in the Soviet Union. We came to this country to be free and did not ever think such things would happen to us."

"What kind of training have these people had?" Stack wanted to know.

"All sorts. Truck drivers, cooks, infantrymen, two tankists."

"I don't have any tanks. Can they use rifles?"

"All of us can. But the Soviets didn't give us much target practice. They build up weapons inventory by not training too much. I was in the Army three years. The last two years I did not even shoot my rifle once."

"Would your people be able to use an M-16 rifle?"

"If you show us."

"Fine. We'll be back at dawn. We have to get more weapons and ammunition. Sorry we can't stay and chat, but time's of the essence."

"I understand," Yusupov said with a smile. Since coming here he had learned to deal with impatient people. No wonder it was such a wonderful, progressive land. Also a strange land. Eight years he had been here and still he didn't understand the place.

He watched the Americans leave and waved good-bye. As they walked off his mind skimmed back across the years to his native land and his city of Rostov on the Don, to the jobs in pipe-manufacturing plants, work as a tractor mechanic, followed by employment in a Kazakhstan gypsum mine near the Iranian border, then a move to Minsk to be near his father's sister. There he had worked in a factory making cotton blouses. All this had led up to his dissident years, his being arrested and shipped off to a labor camp in the Kola Peninsula not far from Murmansk, Finland, and the Arctic Circle. He had planned many escapes which never materialized, till he had been released as part of an amnesty program and allowed to emigrate to Israel during one of the Soviet Union's attempts to get some agreement with the West. He had stayed in Israel nine months, found it not to his liking, and come to New York. From there, he had moved to California, settled a while in L.A., then moved north on the advice of one of his friends who'd said jobs were better and more plentiful in San Francisco. Once there, he had found the place fascinating, disgusting, and beautiful. All at the same time. Part of the puzzle called America.

7

They returned first to the ruined cellar complex, honking to let the sentries know they were coming. As they arrived, people hurried out from below and Galoris began tossing them packs of cigarettes. The crowd grabbed for them like kids being showered with presents by Santa on Christmas night. That's what the war had done, Stack realized, making people glad for the small things, changing their values overnight. Then Galoris briefly left the van to speak to Joy Church and Janet Kagle over on the side, telling them what had gone down. He looked back at the van, where Stack and Courtner waited. They had places to go and things to do. Another visit to Candlestick Park being among them, to tell Colonel Callister what had been learned and arranged so he could give them more weapons.

Galoris finished what he had to say to the women and returned to the van. Then, in a puff of whitish exhaust, they were gone. The people outside talked and smoked their newly opened cigarettes, enjoying themselves for the moment, forgetting briefly the dismal present and the uncertain future. The orange tips of their lit cigarettes danced in the night like lightning bugs. Bright enough to be seen hundreds of yards distant. But only minor additions to the hundreds of firelights across the convoluted hide of this once great city.

A hundred yards to the north, hidden, except for his exposed eyes and upper face, Tim Worrell, one of Yahzdi's foreward scouts, watched, clutching the double-barrel 12-gauge shotgun he had picked up in the ruins of the sporting-goods store which had supplied Yahzdi and his force with rifles, shotguns, pistols, knives, and axes. Some guns were completely destroyed, others were only damaged and able to be repaired after an hour or two of work. This find had left them the best-armed men in the city, or so Worrell believed. He was a weasely-looking, brown-haired man with a prominent nose that too often was into the business of others. His hair was straggly and thinning, his face now soot-smeared, his eyes watchful and unkind. But they had always been that way. Unkind eyes in an unkind life. He had been lying there, watching the encampment, wondering if this was the right place. Then he saw the armed sentries outside. This was the right place. The people who came out were unarmed, mostly women and kids. This would be a piece of cake. He believed that with all his heart.

As he lay there watching, his mind swept back twenty years to his first date. He didn't know why he was remembering it now. Maybe, in their moments of darkness and great tension, men thought about the things that had affected them most. And for many it was their relationship with women. The ones they'd won, lost, or never had. The images of that date welled up from below. A blind date it had been. A fiasco. The girl, after setting eyes on him, had almost gone into convulsions. She couldn't stomach the sight of him. And the worst part was that there had been others there to witness it and talk about it later to make his humiliation worse. It hadn't been the first bad reception he'd received in life and it wouldn't be the last. Eventually he'd learned to cope with it, to advance despite the obstacles on his horizon. But it had hurt. Why all of it had come out here and now he didn't know. But that was the past. All that mattered was who'd be alive tomorrow to see the rising of the sun across the rubble desert of the city.

Worrel had ten men. More than enough people, he judged, to make a successful attack. He could have gone back and reported to Yahzdi and asked for more men, or perhaps let Yahzdi do the leading. But not this time. Tonight he'd be the man of decision, the man of action, the man in charge he'd dreamed of being all his life. He'd lead in the attack, win the battle, then return to Yahzdi and maybe get a promotion. Or, if Yahzdi got too big for his britches, Tim Worrell could take the Americans away with him and lead his own force. This was a new world. A place of opportunity where the strongest gun, the fastest mind, the hardest man would win and be in charge. And if anything stood in his way, Worrell would mow it down. Yeah, he'd be the person he could have become if not for certain circumstances that had prevented him from reaching the level that should have been his in life. With that in mind, he moved along the rubble barrier he was hidden behind toward the next man in line, Louis Maitlin. Maitlin, a small, wiry, black-haired man, looked up from his eyeball reconnaisance of the area and opened his mouth. "What?"

"We're going in. I've decided to attack." For one moment Maitlin's face filled with surprise. This changed to a look of disappointment, as if had started to enjoy just lying there, like a cat hidden in the bushes, studying the goings-on of the world—or like a man enjoying a leisurely meal of steak and french fries, then, just as he gets to the best part, being told he's wanted back at the office pronto and being forced to wolf down the food, not really tasting or enjoying it, mad as hell, but scared for his tail, vowing to himself that next time he'd make up for this by eating an ever bigger, better meal in a still more leisurely fashion.

"Are you sure it's okay? Yahzdi might not like it."

"Let me worry about that. No need to go to Yahzdi. We have enough people to do what needs to be done."

Maitlin had a worried, unsure look on his face. Worrell did not wait for his reactions, but moved on to the next man in line. Louis Attaliyah, an American-born Arab. Tall, balding, with a big beer belly, Attaliyah hiked Worrell's idea. He was hungry for action. There hadn't been enough of it. Instead, there'd been too much talk, false bravado, and laughter that hid great fears. Now they knew exactly where their enemies were. Maybe not all of them. But enough. It was time to act. Attaliyah's assent gave Worrell the courage to convince the others of the correctness of his intent. Among them was Cowboy Bob, who had been a rodeo rider in his younger days—hence the nickname, and Rough Trade, a waterfront tough who liked to wear leather, though his present outfit was somewhat frayed, and go around beating up gays to maintain his own fear-filled, tenuous hold on manhood.

When he finished briefing the others of his intent, the eyes of the men in the group hardened and their faces lost the neutral look of watchers, to be replaced by the slitting of eyes, the near-raising of ears, the clenching of teeth, the thinning of lips, and the tighter clutch of rifles, pistols, and shotguns. It was time to fight. Thinking about combat was one thing. Doing it was a whole other ballgame.

Worrell led the line forward, advancing slowly, moving from behind one obstacle to the next, using the cloak of night to the utmost possible advantage. Rough Trade, moving directly behind, aped his careful movements. Each man there was using what he had learned in his past life about how to advance on an enemy who waits unknowingly for death to emerge from the darkness. They moved with a fair amount of skill. Soldiers without an army. Troops without military experience, except for the few who'd been in the service and were reliving a past so far away it was like a haze on the horizon of their tormented souls. They tried to recall old techniques, which oozed out of the past like rusted winches slowly playing out the the rope the fisherman needs as he tries to lay the nets that will bring in his catch.

Worrell proceeded till he was less than 30 yards from the enemy encampment, then looked back at the pasty-white faces of the men just behind, recognizing the sick look on Attaliyah's face, the grim smile on Cowboy Bob's lips, the worry lines on this face or that. It didn't matter. Soon, the killing would begin and they'd fight—like it or not. Worrell almost instinctively knew that on the battlefield a man doesn't fight for his country or beliefs as much as he fights for his life. The more of your enemies that died, the fewer your chances of joining them.

He hunkered down a moment, knowing the others were waiting for his instructions, yet holding back, not allowing them to rush him, studying what was out there, trying to decide on the best attack pattern to follow. But he could feel their eyes burn into him. The pressure was too great. It was time to make his move. Worrell turned around and began assigning men to positions, planning to catch the enemy in a circle of attackers, whispering to each man he sent out to wait till he fired first and to meanwhile pick out a victim so that when the firing began, he could blast the hell out of the target. Each man nodded silently and went to do his bidding. Worrell now felt a bit more like a commander and slightly surer of himself, his plans, and his future.

Out in front of the cellar complex people were still smoking, talking, smiling, and laughing. Some of the half-dozen sentries guarding the approaches to the area had relaxed a bit and also taken out their cigarettes to have a smoke. One of them, Raussenbush, had even put down his M-16 so he could relax still more. Phelan, the sentry farthest out, almost into the rubble field on the right, stood with a cigarette in his mouth, both hands on his rifle, eyes warily scanning the scene ahead, not being distracted by the merriment of those behind him. But he was the only one so vigilant as the enemy moved carefully and methodically to various points, forming a tight circle around the position.

Worrell watched the dim forms of his men closing the noose slowly and glee filled him at how smoothly all of it was going. Good. Excellent. Soon, very soon, the trap would be sprung and the killing would begin. A sinister joy filled Worrell. He had never killed a man . . . or a woman in his life and wondered how it would feel. The fire in his guts grew. This was the most exciting sensation he'd ever had. It was greater than hunting animals. A hundred, no, a thousand times better. This was followed by sudden thumping of his heart. At first he thought it was due to the excitement, then recognized the flurried heartbeats for what they were. Fear, cold, heart-clenching, gut-gripping fear coming from down deep. Somewhere inside was a gremlin which doubted he could be the man he was pretending to others that he was. But Worrell pushed that gremlin aside. Nothing, but nothing, would tear him from doing what needed to be done.

The men were almost in place as Worrell sat on his fears like a lid atop a volcano and looked out at the people milling about in front of the cellar complex, all the while wondering how deep it went and how large it was. Soon he'd know. He smiled again, more grimly this time as he aimed his shotgun at a group of women and children. Might as well make that first blast count. Let the others take down the armed guards.

He hesitated only a second before pressing down on the trigger, fearful that some vestige of conscience he had left would rear up and intrude on his determination. As he pressed down on the twin triggers of the shotgun the air in front of him exploded in a flash of yellow-red that cut through the darkness and seemed to jump ten feet out ahead of the gun on a host of enraged metallic pellets which grew into a wide swath during their flight to the target. Almost an instant later came the screams of horror as people began to fall, like the cries of a bird caught in the shadow of a downward diving hawk in the fraction of a second before harsh, curving claws knife into flesh and rip the throat and life out of the convulsing body.

Amid the screams and blood-curdling cries of pain torn from victims as pellets struck home, people folded and hands flew up to protect heads and faces while blood spurted from pierced bodies and the wounded grabbed at gashes ripped open by metal entering at supersonic speed. This horror was now magnified when gunfire and shot-

gun blasts erupted in a circle all around the perimeter.
More people grabbed themselves and crumpled to the
ground never to rise again under their own power. Some
others ran in panic for the steps that would take them
down into the cellar complex. As they did so, those
supposed to protect them either dived for cover or moved
forward to the attack. Phelan, the sentry most forward,
spotted two places from which fire splashed, lifted his
rifle, threw off the safety, his mouth simultaneously
opening in a grimace of horror while the lit cigarette he
held fell from his parted lips, sparking as it struck the
earth, before he pressed down on the trigger, firing at the
first target he had seen in short spurts that sent pinkish
flames and plumes of white smoke jerking from the
dancing black barrel as rounds like maddened hornets
winged their way across the short distance between him
and the first attacker. And then he swung his gun in a half
arc toward the next flash he had seen, but the gun out there
boomed first and rubble to Phelan's left flew upward,
some of the chips striking him, stinging as they ricocheted
off in another direction. He paid them no mind as he sent a
flurry of answering rounds flying outward, striking the
second man, some of the bullets richocheting off the
enemy gun with metallic pings. The man screamed, then
went down and back as jets of blood flew off in all
directions. Phelan now wondered if he'd hit the first man
he'd fired at. He'd been turning too fast to try to strike the
second target to notice whether or not he'd hit the first
shooter. Just then he felt an answering round strike home.
For a fraction of a second he thought it was the sting of
some flying rock.

But then he began to fold as deep, digging metal mixed
with a spreading warmth and wetness in his midsection.
Time quickly slowed down for Phelan, who bent over
farther and farther, seeing his boots, watching the M-16
fall in slow motion from now limp fingers as his face went
numb, while the night drew darker, the shooting, shouting,
and screaming weaker. And then a second round went in.

He could feel the pain like a great flash traveling out across the suddenly massive expanse of his body, inside which he saw himself as a smaller and smaller being, while the length and breadth of his form changed and became more a part of the surrounding world, no longer connected to him, a separate place that turned step by step into stone and darkness and an unfeeling strangeness.

Phelan's consciousness fell deeper within, seeing his insides, feeling the second bullet, but not as strong as the first, followed by a flash of warmth racing through him. Then his body pivoted as it was turned, but not under its own power. Being moved instead by the energy of the round that had slammed into him.

Phelan sank deeper now into the endless well that had appeared all around. The sounds? The sounds? Where had they gone? And what of the flashing lights of the firing guns? There was darkness all around. Cold, chilling darkness. He was alone for one long moment. But then he saw the light—a great, white, luminescent ball—and began to move toward it, going faster now, his arms outstretched, black against the blinding whiteness. He had to move toward it. He did not know why. But he had to get there. Some knowledge told him this was the right path. Then, at the edge of the luminescent sphere, he saw people he hadn't seen in years. Jerome, his childhood friend. But Jerome had drowned when he was 12. Phelan was puzzled. Then he saw Jayne, his sister, who'd died last year in a car accident in Colorado. It couldn't be. Both were dead. Phelan next saw his grandfather and mother. And then he understood and smiled and hurried toward the white sphere.

And while Phelan was falling to earth and more bullets were striking him, others were falling too. Tom Grushin, who'd helped defend the B-52 in the mountains, along with some women and children on the southern approach, joined Phelan.

Joy Church, who'd been below when the shooting began, rushed topside and tried to get people to come inside. But too many had panicked and run in all directions, like a chicken with its head cut off. Made madder by the ping of bullets, the crackle of rifles, the roar of shotguns, and the flashes of fire coming from all directions out of the greater night. And each sound was magnified in the almost deathly stillness of the ruined city, echoing across the ruins, growing fainter the farther out it moved along the deserted streets.

"The horror of it, the horror of it," Janet Kagle thought as she ran from behind one rubble pile to the next. There were answering booms from inside the perimeter, and the sounds of them raced through the air as they danced in her stomach and made her heart pound faster than at almost any time in her life. No horror she had imagined, except for the explosion of the bombs, was as great as the present hell, which brought back the searing terror of the bombs going off, the rush of heat, light and superstorm winds that sucked out all the oxygen, creating a firestorm as air raced in from outlying areas, causing great whirlwinds of fire which added to the hells of the explosions, the falling buildings, and the blasts of burning cinders that sucked the life out of people, lifted victims off the streets, and smashed them against walls, breaking their bones as if they were cheap, wooden dolls crushed by wanton children.

A round slammed into the pile she was hidden behind and sent a shower of small pieces of brick flying, filling her nostrils with the sour smell of cleaved rock. And then the panic inside her exploded and she rose to run for some safer pile of debris. She didn't know which one, but it had to be away from here, which seemed to be the most unsafe place in the world, as if everyone were firing at her. And the feeling was further reinforced by the heavy, incoming fire from all directions.

She rose and took no more than half a dozen steps before a shotgun boomed somewhere off to the left and a hornets' swarm of pellets chopped into Janet Kagle, piercing her from the neck down to the abdomen, ripping open a gash along her throat so that the skin hung down by a flap, the pellets also digging into her collarbone, piercing her breasts and to a lesser degree her abdomen and arms, some of them ricocheting and cracking the thick lenses of her glasses. She recoiled both from the impact and shock as the shower of hot, stinging bits of metal smashed into her, their power dissipated somewhat by the distance they had to travel as the enemy moved back under the volume of fire poured out by the defenders.

For half a second she told herself this was all a delusion, a bad, bad dream, that it couldn't be happening. But then she tried to take a step forward and a leg went out from under her as Janet Kagle sat down hard on the uneven, debris-covered ground, her legs sprawled out in front of her before she fell back, aware now that blood was pouring out of her and also leaking inside. Suddenly, she was gasping, trying to swallow blood and breathe at the same time, feeling the sticky, red, rubbery-tasting liquid running down her throat the way it had when she had nosebleeds as a child. But this time the flow was too great and her heart began to pound in terror. She tried to speak, gasping out words, but found that she was just spitting blood, which ran across her lips, then down her chin.

Before she could cry again for help, Raussenbush, one of the biker sentries, ran over, grabbed her under the armpits from behind, and, under heavy fire, while hunkering down, dragged her away from there, getting Janet Kagle behind some ruins. But she was now drowning in her own blood, in danger of suffocating, and this really panicked her, making Janet gasp and fight the flood as she tried to sit up, unable to communicate the horror within and the need to breathe as Raussenbush tried to calm her, finally seeing the wide-eyed look of panic in her eyes as he attempted to get her to lie back and relax. But that made breathing more difficult. And the gasping attempts to get air made her chest heave up and down with greater violence and faster motions. As it did so, the wounds in her chest and lacerated breasts bled harder, turning the ripped, dirty, brown sweater she wore a dark purple-red. But Janet

Kagle did not care. She had to breathe. She needed to talk
and spit out the blood in her mouth, then the blood filling
her throat and the blood she was coughing up constantly.
She began to convulse, and Raussenbush tried to support
her as about a third of a cupful of blood flew from her
mouth in a minor tidal wave that poured out over her
chest, painted her lips red, stained her teeth, and dribbled
down her chin. She tried to talk, but it sounded like the
mumblings of a person with some disease which kept them
from speaking clearly, or the words of a very drunken
woman.

"Relax, relax, relax," he kept repeating, not knowing
what else to do, looking around in panic for someone who
could help and perhaps take this burden off his shoulders.
All the while he reminded himself to hunker down least he
too be shot.

When the firing had first started up, those inside the
cellar complex had looked up in the semi-darkness, the
flames of the fire below dancing across their troubled
features. Then one of them, Vance Chickering, had said,
"What the hell are we waitin' for? Let's get our guns and
asses out there."

As men grabbed for their guns and extra ammo clips,
bumping into one another in the process, panicked people
had charged down from upstairs. The bikers had had to
stand aside as wild faces and open, gasping mouths raced
past, women dragging children, rushing for the safety of
the sewer tunnel below.

Despite this, Chickering was the first to make it topside.
What he saw out there were people sprawled on the
ground. Some dead, others wounded, a few crying, many
just gasping in fear, trying to stem the blood flowing from
their wounds. And then he was spotted and rounds began
to fly his way. Chickering threw himself backwards in
response, smashing into another biker coming up behind
him. "Back, back," Chickering gasped. "The fire's too
heavy. We'll have to wait for it to let up some before we
can do our thing."

Elsewhere, Ty Boozerton gave as good as he got and better. Being the most aggressive of the sentries, he did not lose his head and panic when the shooting began. Boozerton had been in the Marines. It had been 15 years since that time, but the training, the discipline, and the lessons stayed with him. Though rusty, when the first volleys came down, he quickly responded by moving into the rubble and the darkness, out of the line of fire, where he'd be harder to spot and closer to the enemy. Close enough to see faces and bodies. Close enough to start busting caps.

One of the first guys he spotted was Vic Maitlin. Boozerton didn't hesitate for one second as he aimed and fired. His shot didn't catch Maitlin, but it caught the gun he was holding and the ricochet got one of the hands holding the gun. Maitlin yelled in horror and pain as he dropped the gun and brought his left hand up in front of his face. One of the digits between his pinky and middle finger was gone. The bone above it, which held the finger attached to the palm, was shattered and covered with red slime. The blood was now gushing out in jerking spasms with each heartbeat that pulsed life-giving liquid through his body. In horror, Maitlin moved back, but not far enough. Boozerton's second round caught him, not exactly where Boozerton wanted because of the darkness and the fact that his target moved. But the round still rammed home with devastating effect, smashing through the collarbone, breaking it, causing Maitlin to gasp as his head swiveled toward the wound and his good hand rose into the air. But just then the searing pain radiating out from the profusely bleeding wound caused his hand to stop halfway and fall back down as his face was twisted by a grimace of agony, while his entire body spasmed and his head shivered as if he'd been struck by 10,000 volts of electricity.

He rose and staggered back. This saved him from being caught by Boozerton's third bullet, which flew past, raising wind that Maitlin at this point in time didn't even feel. And then he hit a low wall which rose to the backs of his knees. He went back over it, falling down, striking the uneven ground with a thud, hitting his head and back as the fires of the damned passed through his wounds and his mouth formed into a hole through which he screamed out his agony to the very heavens so that some of his compatriots had to look up from their firing.

"Jesus, Mary, mercy, Holy Ghost, Joseph, mercy, shit, oh shit, oh Shit, oh God. The pain, the pain, ahhhhhhhh!" But the men in his group paid little attention to the fallen and kept firing, knowing they were fighting for their very lives.

The screaming reached one woman lying on the ground amid a circle of wounded children. She looked badly injured, but did not think her wounds very serious. Mostly subsurface pellet penetration. Yet she lay there, as did the children—on her advice—none of them moving, hoping the enemy would think they were dead and therefore out of all this and no longer any threat, as if they had ever been one.

All across the perimeter others, not yet wounded, were able to concentrate on the battle going on around them, and prayed harder than they had ever prayed in their lives for this to be over and for them to make it out of there alive. One of them remembered the saying that there weren't any atheists on the battlefield. She didn't know if it were true, but she said a lot of things in her mind she hadn't said in a long time.

In the circle surrounding the encampment Worrell was reloading his gun, sweating profusely all the while, scared to death. He'd fired a ton of shells, but doubted he'd hit anyone after the first volley, and had almost been hit twice himself. Goddamn, but this was a scary piece of business. It was time to take stock and see who was still alive and who'd been hit. That decided, Worrell began to crawl from firing position to firing position, calling out to each man in a loud whisper that it was him so they wouldn't by mistake shoot their commander.

He got plenty of grit on himself and swallowed a few cupfuls of dust, but that couldn't be helped. Nobody said war was a picnic. And the longer this siege went on, the more he understood the war weariness of professional soldiers who wanted like hell to stay away from the battle-field each time they had a taste of it. But stay they did. For many till the bitter end.

The firing continued intermittently as Vance Chickering and Victor Bonalilla joined the battle. Bonalilla in particular hated this. Dying in such a vile place for Nortes was not the most appealing thing in his mind at that moment. Had there been a way out, he would have gotten on his motorcycle and ridden the hell out of there, heading down to Mexico, which surely hadn't been hit, and merging with the populace to do his part in building up that country now that America was down the drain, or pretty much there anyhow.

Worrell reached Maitlin, who kept groaning. "Easy, guy, easy," Worrell gasped. "They'll hear you and that'll draw fire."

Maitlin put a lid on it, but still gasped out in a much too loud voice, "Get me the fuck out of here. I'm hurt—hurt bad. You got us the fuck into this, you get us the fuck out of this."

"I'll do it. I'll do it, man. Just give me time to get this organized."

"Get it fuckin' organized now," Maitlin gasped. "Quick, before none of us is left to walk out of here."

"Yeah, yeah. Hold on. I'm going to talk to the others." Worrell then crawled away, glad to be gone from the wounded, viper-tongued Maitlin, wondering if there were more like him. But in crawling off he exposed too much of himself, and a flurry of shots streaked his way, a number of them signaled by flaming tracer rounds.

Worrell hugged the ground and ate dust as bullets thunked into this spot or that, chewing rock or concrete or brick, ricocheting off metal. And then, as the fire abated somewhat, he moved out like some insect skittering across wind-rippled sand, hoping to make it behind cover before another flurry came down.

Worrell recalled a time, years ago, when he had lived in a seedy part of town, in a rooming house infested with roaches, and how sometimes during the day a roach would race across the floor and under a newspaper as Worrell walked into the room. But Worrell had seen it and would race across the floor and bring his foot down hard on the newspaper so that the roach underneath, surprised by this sudden and unexpected attack—assuming roaches, like people, can be surprised—died a quickly and probably only briefly painful death. Some roaches did not depend on subterfuge and made a run for it when he appeared. Some made it, others didn't. Worrell always felt great satisfaction when he triumphed in these uneven contests wherein victory for him meant death for the roach. Wherein the roach could never kill him. Where in the roach had to match its primitive brain against his more evolved mind, its small size moving at top speed across what to it was an endless plain of wood or linoleum, against his long legs, its inability to see, depending on feelers, against his ability to scan the entire room in under two seconds. His height advantage in seeing, versus its floor-level vista. What amazed him was that roaches got away so often. But now these thoughts were not such fun, because he was the roach and out there the men firing the guns had much harsher weapons then he had used against roaches. And while those devices didn't squash, they tore, ripped, lacerated, and mangled. Nor was this any longer like hunting. It may have been more exciting, but the hunted could turn into hunters and they were often as intelligent as, if not more intelligent than, their trackers.

Worrell made it to the next man in line. Rough Trade. And Rough Trade was in no mood to stop. "Can't talk now, chief," he gasped in the middle of a hard and heavy firefight with two bikers. He was using a reconditioned Lee-Enfield .303 caliber, bolt-action rifle that the owner of the looted hunting shop had been turning into a sport weapon. Accurate, able to kill out to 2800 yards, the Lee-Enfield, pride of the British Army in World War I and World War II, was now laying out a deadly tattoo of fire that pinned the defenders down almost as often as they pinned him down.

Finally, Rough Trade decided to do a little damage to their bikes, which were parked off to one side and had not been the object of any combat action so far. Three bullets laced into Bonalilla's bike, sending pieces of metal flying. He cursed hot Spanish curses, reared up, and tried to catch Rough Trade in his arc of fire. And Rough Trade, noticing this sudden flare-up, knew whose bike he'd hit and quickly reloaded, shifting his attention and aim toward Bonalilla. Rough Trade's first round sent up a spume of dust to Bonalilla's left. The next round came closer and forced the biker to stop firing. He let his rifle drop to the ground, hunkered down, and ate dirt as he tried to shimmy behind cover, but was afraid to move too much as rounds came closer and closer.

Fire from other defenders who were not pinned down or diverted by fire from elsewhere laced into the position occupied by Rough Trade, who merely laughed nervously as Worrell moved away. Rough Trade dropped down, then popped up to fire into the perimeter from a point ten feet away. More puffs of dirt shot up around Bonalilla, now glued to the ground, unable to move, the fear inside him dancing like maddened waves on a storm-swept sea. He felt like the man who'd waited too long to get into the stock market and now, while all hell breaks loose and everyone around him makes money is afraid to get in too late, just before it is all over, yet is tempted to move, but unsure, not knowing in which direction to go, trying to avoid the flack flying every which way.

But this was a lot harder than failing in the market. Failure here meant maiming or death. Worrell now joined the battle and blasted away twice with his shotgun. The second blast caught Bonalilla squarely across the upper chest. He grimaced in pain, then, with a loud "arrgh," lifted up. That was all Rough Trade needed as he fired twice, fast, one shot after the other, both of them striking home. Bonalilla spasmed visibly as each round went into him, then twisted left and right before falling back down, bleeding profusely, his lungs and right arm pierced. "Help me, heeelp me," he gasped as he rapidly bled to death, and shivers of shock passed along his form from the recoil effect of the rounds that had penetrated his flesh. This was followed by numbing and a surge of heat from the wound centers. Quickly, breathing became harder as a sensation of wetness filled his insides. Bonalilla was aware of the blood dripping out of his body and tried to will it to stop. No, not his good, clean blood dripping out onto the dirty, ruined earth. But after a few seconds he realized his foolishness. No man, thought Victor Bonalilla, except for a yoga perhaps, could will wounds to stop bleeding. Then he realized that not even a yoga could stop such wounds from leaking. A series of chills, mixed with waves of heat, passed through him. He felt great drops of cold sweat across his face and wanted to lift a hand to wipe them away. Bonalilla tried to lift his right arm, but it wouldn't move, and the effort merely sent a surge of bright, purple pain through him so that he had to shut his eyes tight as more great drops of cold sweat appeared on his face. Next, Bonalilla tried to move his left arm. But it wouldn't move either. He wondered why. It hadn't been hit. Out of curiosity he tried moving his legs. Nothing. Had his spinal cord been hit? Bonalilla tried to move the rest of his body and felt nothing. Then he tried to identify where he was wounded. But there was no sensation. Even in his face. Bonalilla should have felt something. He should have, but he didn't. Dammit! He saw nothing now. His eyes were open, but there were no images. He tried to blink his eyes and shake his head, yet the darkness did not go away. Suddenly, he began to see scenes from his childhood. Himself at the age of two. A fat, brown baby. His parents smiling, laughing, playing with him. In his mind, Bonalilla smiled. Then he saw himself at age seven climbing into the

treehouse he had built, holding his pet cat, Little Tiger. A
face appeared, replacing the other scene. The face of his
former wife, smiling now, calling to him, her hair platinum
blonde like the pale gold he had always dreamed the Norte
princess he someday took would wear. She was calling him
by the pet name she had used before times had become bad
for them, before they had separated and divorced. Did all
the images he was seeing mean he was dead? Dead? Why
would he ask that? And then Victor Bonalilla thought no
more and his body lay silent on the crushed ground, the
dust underneath him drinking up his coagulating blood
like the sand on an abattoir floor.

But all around him there was no peace. The night was
rent by pink and orange and blue flashes and men
screaming either from being hit, or out of fear, as they
called out to this or that buddy to watch it amid calls for
aid.

Worrell finished his circuit of the combat line and discovered that three of his people were now dead. Maitlin
was wounded and the remaining six were okay and still
fighting. But they weren't winning this war. Dammit!

Vance Chickering was now moving forward, slamming
into the enemy. He fired a number of times, but hit no one.
That didn't bother him. He'd get lucky sooner or later. All
he needed was time to orient himself. He was aware,
despite his inexperience, that this had degenerated into an
all-out firefight with no one directing the defenders. But
why should anyone direct them? Their leaders, Courtner
and Stack, weren't here.

Unable to influence events in the confused and hellish
firefight, Chickering did the best he could, adding his two
cents' worth to the battle. He spotted someone moving out
from behind cover 40 yards away and let off a flurry of
shots on automatic. An enemy fighter arched as the bullets
caught him, lacing into the foe from belly to head, sending
blood spurting in all directions as the man crumpled to the
ground dead.

Chickering rose and ran to a pile of smashed wood and

bricks 20 feet away. As he did so, a flurry of shots followed him, the ground behind him erupting in tiny pillars of dust and debris. But Chickering made it behind the mound, throwing himself down on the sharp-edged rubble, his heart beating rapidly, more from fear than exertion, his eyes wild with the knowledge of what those bullets could have done had they struck home.

Worrell was not among those doing the firing. He was still moving from place to place, counting his losses. Another man dead. That made four, and Maitlin mangled. Shit and piss. What was he going to do? A small voice from within called out, "Get the fuck outta here, dude." Yeah, that's it. He'd get out. Call this a soft probe which bloodied the enemy and tested his strength. Then tell Yahzdi what a great thing they'd done. He'd buy it. Worrell crawled over to Louis Attaliyah.

"Louie, Louie," he whispered. "It's time to get the hell outta here. They're too strong. This is gonna hafta end as a soft probe."

"Sure. Anything you say. I'll start pulling back," Attaliyah agreed, never having been so scared in his life, except for the nuclear attacks, which he still hadn't gotten over.

"Not yet, not yet," Worrell shot back. "Wait till I give the order. If we pull back too soon, they'll surge forward and we'll all be slaughtered." With that, he crawled to the next man in line, making his slow circuit of the attack circle, which was now as full of holes as a piece of swiss cheese.

Cowboy Bob, who'd fought in Vietnam, wasn't worried and not much impressed by the intensity of the battle. His mind kept moving from now to the past and back again in a rubber-band reaction so that the fiery flash of shots in the darkness and the sight of swift, skittering figures were mixed with combat scenes from Vietnam. Scenes of blocks ravaged by combat in the cities. Houses full of hidden Vietcong or NVA troops as Americans moved up endless streets or lay behind burned out vehicles and damaged troop carriers for protection while supporting armor moved up or stood like immobile monoliths, firing occasional shells into this building or that, the rooms of which came apart in a flash of reddish fire and billowing black smoke and flying parts of bodies. Sometimes, the tanks would stand there firing volley upon volley of machine-gun rounds into a structure while troops moved forward, shooting into various houses, slowly taking back block after painful block which the Communists had grabbed in one of their endless offensives. Wary-eyed troops entered buildings, shooting and being shot at. What a hell that had been. This was nothing like it. Cowboy Bob fired another flurry of rounds at a defender trying to move from behind one mound to a better position and missed. Godamnit! But then he swung the rifle on wounded civilians lying in front of the underground complex and fired indiscriminately, thinking to himself that he was blasting the hell out of future faggots, faggot supporters, or degenerates of some kind. Several kids spasmed as his bullets sliced into them. After a few twitches they moved no more.

Chickering saw what happened, cursed, looked for the source of the firing, thinking to himself that these bastards had no mercy, no sense of right or wrong. This war, like any other, brought out the worst in men. The most rancid shit, killers of the most despicable kind, rose to the surface. And vermin like that couldn't be allowed to float around as they burned, crushed, and destroyed whatever they wanted till their filthy bloodlust was satisfied. This garbage had to be eliminated now. And the sooner, the better. Till this point Chickering had merely reacted, going into this for the hell of it, to help his buddies meet a commitment and to follow the orders of Colonel Callister. But now, for the first time, Chickering vowed with the very insides of his heart and soul to finish off these disgusting sons of bitches.

Watching the fighting, Worrell for the first time felt a great weariness as his nerves began to give him trouble.

Like a black worm at the back of his mind, a nagging worry filled him that this might not end as he had planned it. That the people defending the perimeter might be able to surge forward and blast the hell out of their attackers. The sparkling fires of the guns reminded Worrell of the sensations he felt and the lights he had seen back in his hometown of Moline, Illinois, when the bartender in his favorite tavern had made up a concoction called Satan's Surprise. And the damned thing had never failed to surprise him. Once or twice it had gotten him into some car accidents he'd been lucky enough to walk away from.

But this was no alcohol-induced stupor. This was the real thing, and a good jolt from one of those guns out there and a man wouldn't ever wake up again. And no cause, not even one from God himself, was worth dying for. At least that's how Worrell felt as he finished informing his men that on his signal they should begin withdrawing. He and Rough Trade would drag Maitlin away. Maitlin, by now, was bleeding like a stuck pig and looked in a bad way, all pale, with his eyes fiery, mouthing strange, frightening thoughts, only half of which were logical, with the rest ending up in mumblings. Worrell was sure Maitlin was going into and out of shock. Goddamn. There had to be a better way of making this plan work. Too bad he'd started the attack. Those hippies certainly hadn't been easy to break. They must've gotten help in the meantime. But from whom? He would find that out in time, he was sure. Worrell knew he'd miscalculated. He should have gone back and reported what he'd seen and let Yahzdi decide on the attack. But it was too late to recall what he'd done. That was all sperm under the bridge, as he was fond of saying. Right now he had to get the hell out of here. And yet, despite the fact that the battle hadn't gone well, he grinned. His attack had wounded the enemy, wounded them badly, and cost them more blood than they'd cost him. And most important of all, it had been other men's blood. Not his.

Worrell called Rough Trade to him and together they

went to get Maitlin. Worrell looked at the badly wounded, muttering, pain-filled Maitlin and told Rough Trade, "You start draggin' him. I'm going to fire the shot that'll tell the others to slowly pull back. Then I'll join you."

"Right," Rough Trade said with that seemingly half-wit smile of his and the gleam in those dark eyes under his overhanging bushy eyebrows. And then, gorilla of a man that he was, he grabbed Maitlin under the armpits and began to drag him.

"Stop, stop, ahhhhh," Maitlin cried out. "Jesus, Mary, and Joseph. The pain, the pain. Stop it. Someone kill this piece of motherfuckin' shit. Please! Kill this piece of shit! Shit must die! Shit must die!" His cries rent the night. Worrell looked back. Louis Attaliyah looked up from his firing. Even those inside the defense perimeter heard what was going on. "Who the hell was that?" Chickering thought. One of the bastards must have been caught by a bullet. But, in the middle of his screaming, Maitlin fainted and the grinning Rough Trade, who had not let up for one moment, pulled Maitlin farther away from the sounds of firing.

Worrell, meanwhile, had reached the cover of a mound, looked out at the motorcycles parked off to one side, and decided to keep the enemy occupied while he and his people made their withdrawal.

Worrell pointed his weapon at the motorcycles, pressed down on both triggers, and gave them everything he had. The roar was deafening. The yellow-orange blast of fire ejected from both barrels split and separated the swift, widening swarm of pellets that they carried, and, at the same time, lit the night, illuminating Worrell's face, causing his hair to fly in the wind for a fraction of eternity as the short distance between his gun and the motorcycles were bridged by the racing pellets, which penetrated rubber, metal, and leather. Tires burst, gas tanks were pierced, windshields were cracked, one machine keeled over and another exploded in a roaring ball of orange flame, shooting debris, black smoke, and sparking bits of burning rubber all over the place. The bikers looked up in surprise. Some of them rose and began running to try and save their valuable bikes. Louis Attaliyah took the opportunity to fire one last time at a particularly trouble-some biker, but still missed.

The defenders, now perfect targets, ran to save their machines before the fires could spread and destroy their only means of transportation. But none of them was getting hit, because their enemies had had enough and were using the chaos to withdraw—not the first time an enemy in time of war had ignored a perfectly good opening because he was too exhausted and had taken too many loses to do anything about the available opportunity.

Worrell moved back the fastest, catching up with the madly laughing Rough Trade and grabbing the legs of the now semi-conscious Maitlin, helping carry him across uneven ground, both men almost tripping every 20 feet, but making it nonetheless, barely feeling the weight of the wounded man because of the tension around them and the high adrenalin flow racing through them.

Those who had withdrawn opened the circle like two arms of a pincer returning to the source from which it had flowed. All of them soon reached the slower-moving Worrell and Rough Trade. A deadening quiet descended around them, except for the gasps and groans of the wounded man and the crunch of their shoes and boots over the rubble of the land.

But back at the perimeter there was pandemonium. Angelicus, Raussenbush, Chickering, Stu Englund, and others were trying to wheel their bikes away, cringing under the flames which grabbed at them, singed their hair, sent sparks all over them, and lit up the night. Some of them, in the haste to save their bikes, had even dropped their rifles, not even remembering where. Each man tried to get his bike. Then, when that proved impossible in the panic, pandemonium, and sheer insanity of the fire, they grabbed any bike and got it out of the way. An explosion threatened any minute, and all of them hurried to get away so that none of them would get splashed by flying fuel. In this they succeeded, though they bumped into one another and had to wheel their heavy bikes around mounds and rubble barriers, knowing that, had they not put up such a hard fight, the enemy would have been able to devote more attention to the bikes earlier and the present disaster would have been much worse.

They moved with a determination and certainty of purpose that was amazing in such a confused situation, like troops in a surrounded pocket, harassed from all sides, under constant air and artillery fire, losing trucks, tanks, jeeps, and armored cars in a steady tattoo of destruction, yet trying to save each and every vehicle so that it could be used in the breakout, leaving nothing to the enemy. And though such attempts rarely achieved their objectives, men still tried. This time, however, they were able to get 11 bikes out of the way, 2 of them substantially damaged, before a burning bike went up in a purple-red luminescent pillar of fire that broke the bike in half, tossing the flaming tires in opposite directions, while a puff of black smoke jetted up as if from some giant's chimney.

Angelicus, shocked at the power of the explosion, thought of what would have happened had he been near it. His bike had been parked only a few yards away. The reality of what might have happened sent a shiver of fear along his spine the same way it had when he'd realized how close to death he'd come in some battle in Vietnam.

Raussenbush, who'd been comforting the badly wounded Janet Kagle, had dropped her cradled head when he'd run to save his endangered bike. Now, he realized what he had done and forgot the bike, rushing back to find her. She was on the ground where Raussenbush had left her, blood all over the place.

"How are you? How are you?" he frantically yelled as he dropped to his knees and lifted her head. Janet Kagle was still gurgling, her eyes now shut, blood pouring from her mouth. She'd been like that during the battle, mumbling words through the blood she was swallowing.

But now she was hardly breathing. He slapped her cheeks, called her name, pulled up her eyelids, and saw that Janet's eyes were up and back. And then she stopped breathing. A tremor passed through Raussenbush. Had she been going over the edge when he still held her? Or did she finally drown in her own blood, no longer able to keep her head up, when he'd dropped her to go for his bike? He didn't know. Had he lost a human being just to save something made of metal and rubber? Raussenbush couldn't answer that either, and his horror-filled face gazed across the perimeter as others lifted their heads now that the shooting had stopped.

8

The van pulled to a stop in front of Candlestick Stadium. Everyone got out and Stack locked up. Then they headed into the stadium, casting a sideways glance at the four quartz-crystal halon searchlights on the truck to their left, the quadruple beams eating into the night, illuminating thin cylinders of the sky for 3000 angled feet in every direction, calling out to the poor, the sick, the homeless, like the Statue of Liberty. "Come. Come to these scattered shores and we will give you solace, help, and hope for the future. But not too much."

The trio headed inside, moving along halls still full of sick and wounded and dying. The load had not gotten any lighter since they had last been here. Going up the hall, they met Doctor Halpin heading in the other direction.

"You here about the two wounded you brought in?" he asked on the run. By now he had passed them and was looking back over his shoulder.

"No. We're here to see Colonel Callister," Stack said. "But how are they?" Doctor Mike, as he was known, wiggled his hand from side to side. "They'll live," he said, and then he was gone.

They reached stairs and headed up into the stadium. Colonel Callister was still there, talking to some men in uniform. The three visitors moved across the open area, now not so open with people sleeping on the ground or aimlessly moving about. Stunned, shocked, lost souls not yet recovered from the horrors of the bombing.

141

The three reached Callister, with Stack in the lead. Despite the darkness and scant illumination, Stack thought he recognized one of the men in khaki standing next to Callister. And then he grinned, the grin extending from ear to ear.

"Bill," he called out, breaking into laughter at the sight of the burly, crewcut, beer-bellied, hard-faced, thick-lipped, cold-eyed major he'd met down in Fresno and with whom he'd done some rescue operations.

"Nick," Major Bill Bathhurst called out. And then they briefly embraced. "Wayne—I mean, Colonel Callister—told me you were here. I arrived just half an hour ago. What's up?" Stack gave him a brief rundown, introduced his companions, then quickly explained to Callister what had gone down since last they met. Stack then laid out his plans and his need for more guns and ammo.

"Need any help, good buddy?" Bathhurst asked.

"You're welcome to join us," Stack said with glee. "But don't you have a family to find?"

"That I do," Bathhurst said, temporary sadness creasing his features. Then he scratched his crewcut head. "But I think I can spare a few hours for a buddy. Even more, if need be."

"If you do that, the least I can do is return the favor and help you find your people."

Bathhurst laughed, stuck out his hand, and said, "Agreed. Let's shake on it." They did, then both grinned and looked at Callister.

"Glad somebody's been making friends," Callister said half sarcastically. Then he looked at Stack. "Now, how many guns do you want?"

"Eight rifles, two thousand rounds of ammo, and two dozen grenades."

"Make it ten rifles," Bathhurst said. "One for me and an extra in case someone else decides to join up and fight. That's almost always the case in situations such as this."

Callister called over an adjutant and ordered him to get these men whatever they needed. As the group headed away, Callister called out after them, "I hope I'll be hearing good news from you damn soon. And the damn sooner, the damn better."

Laughing, Stack answered, "We'll do our level best to see to it that your faith in us is rewarded, sir."

"Glad to hear that. Go to it and bring me a victory I'll be proud of."

Stack wanted to ask if he'd get a medal for it, but thought better of opening his mouth and followed the adjutant down to the same room they'd been in earlier in the day.

When they had what they needed, the men staggered back to the van with their heavy cargo. Once everything had been loaded up, they thanked the adjutant, got into the van, and drove away, moving in silence through the enveloping darkness, the overwhelming ruins of a great city and the endless bonfires across the night having their effect. Each man rode along inside his own world, wondering about the present as well as the days far ahead and where their bones might bleach on some strange tomorrow.

After huffing, puffing, and taking turns carrying Maitlin, who occasionally woke from his stupor, cried out in pain, and fainted once more, then reached their base. It was now closely guarded by many armed men. Worrell called out to one of them. "Browne, Browne, it's me, Worrell."

"Yo, Worrell. What's happenin' baby?" the other man called back in a fairly jovial tone, his big belly wobbling, as he came toward them. But then he saw what they were carrying and that the group was smaller than the one that had gone out.

He ran forward. "What the hell happened?"

"We found an enemy encampment, made an attack, and wounded them badly. But they were too damn powerful for us, so we had to withdraw. Go tell Yahzdi."

"Yeah, right." Browne stood there a second, rooted to

the ground, then turned and ran back into the HQ complex. He moved through the maze of roofless halls, finding his way in the dim illumination to the central chamber, where the fires were going and Yahzdi and his lieutenants were.

Browne burst in breathless and quickly related what had happened. Yahzdi, without saying anything, sudden concern in the bright fires of his eyes, raced from the room, past Browne, Farouky on his heels. Others joined them and raced outside to where Maitlin was now on the ground with the survivors of the battle and a cornered Worrell looking down at him. As Yahzdi rushed up, Worrell began talking, excusing himself and explaining away the losses. Yahzdi heard only one word in ten till his mind began focusing on the flurry of words shooting from the black, moving hole that was Worrell's mouth. He had suspected this man was an idiot and Worrell had proven himself tonight.

Yahzdi held up a hand for silence. Worrell shut up, but only momentarily. Yahzdi began to ask questions and Worrell explained about the attack, where it had gone down, his losses and those of the enemy.

"Did they have many men with guns?" he asked, cutting to the important details.

"Yes, many. More than I expected when we attacked."

"How many?"

"It was impossible to count. There was so much firing and it was too dark. But it could have been as many as two dozen fighters. They suddenly came out from underground, unexpectedly."

"I see." Yahzdi walked back and forth worriedly. "Any other places like this one?"

"It's the only one I know about."

Yahzdi walked back and forth a few more times, nodded, then said, "Okay. We will deal with this. But first, we must get this man," he pointed to Maitlin, "some medical attention. He must be taken to the medical emergency center in Candlestick Park."

"How will we carry him that far, sir?"

"Not carry, you fool," Yahzdi spat. "There are some cars covered by rubble not far from here. We'll remove the rubble, see which one is mechanically fit, jump-start it, and drive the man there."

"Very good, sir. I will get some men and go do this immediately." Worrell hurried away. Yahzdi watched his back and thought to himself that this idiot had caused the first defeat to be inflicted on the group. Under Yahzdi's direction the whole group operated as a team. And a force so large could not be defeated. But he had sent an idiot on a wise man's mission. Like trying to get a camel through the eye of a needle.

As the van approached the vicinity of the cellar complex, the four men inside sensed something was very wrong. Stack slowed to a crawl. He pulled his gun closer to him, and then spotted the first smoke and fire flashes going off into the sky above the cellar complex. Stack put on the brakes, then cut the motor and in a low voice said to the other three, "Me and Bill here," he looked at Bathhurst, "are going to go forward to check things out. You wait here with the van. Something's not kosher out there."

"Sure," Galoris said, worry in his voice and sudden tension across his face as the two men got out, each holding an M-16. They moved steadily through the wastes off the road until they got within visual range of the cellar complex.

Stack was about to go over a mound when he felt something softer than rubble beneath his feet. Looking down, he saw a body, and pointed it out to Bathhurst. Both men immediately went into a crouch and eyeballed the surrounding terrain before Stack looked down and examined the dead man. He wasn't one of theirs. An enemy attacker? It looked like it. Stack eyeballed the double-barreled shotgun lying next to him. None of his people had such a weapon. And it had been left behind. This told him the enemy had attacked, been given a rough reception, and hastily withdrawn. Stack and Bathhurst rose and began to move forward again. As they did, both spotted another body with a Lee-Enfield rifle lying alongside it. They moved on, leaving the gun, advancing over a rise just ahead. On coming over it they saw the clearing in front of the cellar complex, the burning bike, the bikes that had been pulled away, the dead and the wounded, the bikers and the members of the commune ministering to the wounded, lots of blood on the bikers. Not all of it their own.

"What the hell's happened?" Stack yelled as he ran forward, followed by Bathhurst.

Joe Angelicus hurried toward him. "We were attacked unexpectedly," he gasped, his eyes wild pinpricks of fire, his mouth an open hole, his chest heaving up and down as he hyperventilated.

Stack didn't have to ask who the attackers were. He looked and saw Raussenbush trying to revive the now dead Janet Kagle, her smashed glasses lying off to one side. Near the entrance to the cellar five or six kids and a woman lay dead or wounded. He saw walking wounded. The place was a mess.

"Wait," he told Bathhurst and Angelicus. "I'll go get the others." He rushed back through the darkness as if he were being carried by wings, stepping on the same body he had stepped on before, but barely feeling it this time, moving right on. When he reached the van, Galoris and Courtner saw by the look on his face that things were not well. He quickly told them all that had happened and then they ran from the van, hurrying alongside him till they got to the clearing.

"My God, what's happened?" Galoris exclaimed when he first laid eyes on everything, though he'd been expecting this. He ran over, knelt down at the side of a woman, talked with her a moment, then rose, ran over to a child, tried to speak to him, but found that the child was in shock. As he stood up he saw Joy Church coming from inside with water to wash the wounds of the injured and ran over to her.

"Are you okay, darling?" he gasped.

"I'm fine. But many of the others aren't. They attacked while you were gone." Tears appeared in her eyes. "It was horrible, horrible. So many killed. To have survived the bombs and radiation, then to have died at the hands of those monsters. What a terrible ending." She began to sob, but forced it down. "I mustn't do that. I must keep control. I must."

Galoris said nothing as his own eyes misted over. The shock of losing so much so soon was getting to him. He tried to keep control of his heart and mind and guts even though he was reeling and his insides were turning to jelly and great drums beat inside his head while vast flashes of light raced past his field of vision. This wasn't as terrible as when the bombs first came down, yet he felt worse. What happened wasn't accompanied by the great cataclysmic forces of the universe which bounced men around so much their insides didn't have time to react and their minds didn't have the space to think. But now he had the time and didn't like what he was thinking or experiencing. But then Stack walked over and Galoris had to focus his vision from within to the world outside.

"They know where we are," he told Galoris. "Things have to be speeded up. We either have to get your people out of here, or build a fortified line inside the cellar complex. At the same time we've got to contact all the people we've already seen, get our volunteers, quickly train them, and make a night assault before the enemy can mount another attack. We might have to attack their HQ, assuming they haven't moved it in the meantime."

"We'll do whatever you say," Galoris answered, his eyes and face troubled.

Stack walked away from him and over to Bathhurst. "The first thing we have to do is get the wounded medical attention. Some of them look pretty bad. We'll get some men to help off-load the guns and ammo we brought. Then we'll load in the wounded and get them outta here."

"But first make sure that every man who can hold a gun is out on the perimeter guarding the approaches to this

place in case those sweethearts decide to come back,"
Bathhurst said. "And not so close in this time. Put them
out in the rubble, among the shadows, where they can have
cover and notice the approach of the enemy more easily."

"Good idea," Stack commented, then indicated he had
to speak to Courtner for a few minutes and walked off.
Courtner and most of his bikers were standing around the
three bodies of their dead compatriots. Some of them
looked as if they wanted to sob, but none did. Courtner's
face was hard and troubled as he looked down at the dead
without saying anything. Stack wondered how much
longer he would stand there, not wanting to disturb his
painful vigil.

Perhaps 30 seconds passed before Courtner noticed
Stack. He looked at him uncomprehendingly at first, then
said, "I didn't know that losing buddies could hurt so
much. That's more pain than I felt when my parents
died."

Stack said nothing, though a lot of sentences and
phrases danced in his head. This was a moment to remain
silent. However, there wasn't the time to be gentle and
considerate. A war was waiting. There were things to be
done and decisions to be made. So Stack began speaking in
a low, even voice, explaining all the deeds that needed to be
done. When he was finished, Courtner nodded and
ordered most of his men into defensive positions. "We'll
bury these guys later," he said. "Right now more urgent
matters intrude."

Stack respected Courtner for holding together and doing
what was needed despite the pressures tugging on his
insides. Those who hadn't been given defensive positions
went to the van to help unload the guns and ammo and
Stack's camping gear to make room for the wounded.
Everyone who didn't have another job joined in this task,
down to the women and children. The attack had formed
them into a common bond. The volunteers carried everything down into the cellar complex, with Courtner joining
them to oversee the storage of the equipment. Stack,

topside, arranged the taking away and loading of the injured. The dead he passed, serene now, slept the sleep of the just and unjust either in a dark void or in a bright, warm, and good place. He didn't know which, and it was a secret only they knew and which they did not reveal to the fearful living. Soon, when all other tasks had been done, they would be placed to rest inside the wounded womb of the earth, oblivious to the suffering, anguish, horrors, and struggles that would continue each summer, fall, winter, and spring until time ceased.

Stack did not dwell long on these things. He got two bikers to carry a badly injured boy, who kept crying out in agony, to the van. Then he ordered a pair of women to help a third female inside. "Those who can sit must do so," he called out. "There isn't room to let everyone lie down."

A dispirited Bushnell appeared at his side. "How can I help?"

Stack pointed to a boy of four or five. "You can carry him. But be careful. He's got an abdominal wound." Bushnell did as asked. Still, the boy cried out when lifted. But then Bushnell whispered something to him. The child nodded, grew silent, put an arm around Bushnell's neck, and was carried off to the van.

The vehicle was quickly loaded up with men, moaning women, and crying children. The press of bodies in the interior, the dripping of blood, the gasping for breath created a fevered atmosphere of despair, pain, and horror. While the other loaders stayed behind, Stack and Galoris got into the van and started off. Though they went slowly and carefully, the van rocked from side to side and bumped up and down over uneven terrain. But this couldn't be helped. The air was soon filled with gasps, groans, cries, and low sobbing. Stack steeled himself and hoped the trip wouldn't be as long as it seemed to be taking.

Mercifully, it didn't last forever. The searchlights, cutting through the darkness above the stadium guided them, Stack arrived at their destination in a short while. He parked, and while Galoris waited with the wounded and tried to comfort them and allay their fears, Stack ran inside, moving down dimly lit halls full of people holding candles, as he looked for a doctor or nurse. Halfway down one hall he ran into an exhausted, dirty, sweat-covered Doctor Halpin and told him about the trouble back at the cellar complex and the wounded outside.

Halpin smiled, shocked amusement in the eyes behind his dirty glasses. "Leave it to Doctor Mike. Let me get some nurses and see about this latest problem. What you're telling me about survivors of the bombings gunning one another down is unbelieveable, I think the radiation's gotten to their brains."

Halpin headed back the way he'd come, leaving Stack standing there, wondering if he should wait for the doctor or go after him. Stack decided to wait. He spent three or four minutes listening to groaning and people having conversations while others deliriously talked about their families, past lives, and events that had happened many years and decades ago. The sounds of many voices speaking at once, not all of them sensibly, the smell of unwashed bodies, festering wounds, and burned flesh which clung to everything made Stack feel as if he were inside the head of some madman suffering from the heat of the noonday sun. But then Doctor Mike came hurrying along with three nurses and some paramedics carrying stretchers. Stack led them outside.

Once back at the van, he opened the rear doors and stepped aside. Doctor Mike poked around, asked questions, checked wounds, then decided who went first, who'd walk, and which ones would be carried. Stack watched as blood dripped down onto the floor of the van, then dripped from the stretchers being carried on the double into the stadium to some impromptu emergency room. Just like a bloody battlefield emergency station. But this wasn't some distant front. This was America. And yet it was a battlefield. The entire planet was now a combat zone. He gasped as the full power of that realization passed through his mind. By then the van was empty as Doctor Mike and his people disappeared into the stadium. Galoris came over to Stack and said, "What do we do now? Wait?"

"What for? They're not coming right back. Those people have been badly wounded. They'll be there for weeks. Some might even die. I know that's not good to hear," he said, looking at the surprise on Galoris's face, "but we've got to get used to some harsh realities. Especially now."

Galoris nodded. "I'm ready. Don't be mistaken about that. I just don't like it."

"Mister, I like nothing about this war. Not one damn thing," Stack said harshly. "But I live with it. Not just one day at a time, but hour by hour and minute by minute. You have no idea, no damn idea of how hard this thing is on me and the strain I have to go through to push down my inner feelings and proceed with this life as if I'm walking across a flat road with no dips or rises in it."

Galoris looked at him and said nothing. Just then a car pulled in about 50 feet away. Two men got out, went to the rear of the car, and pulled out a groaning man who was bleeding badly. Worrell and Rough Trade carried him double-time into the stadium. Stack and Galoris, not knowing who they were, watched this. Stack lit up a smoke while Galoris, curious about the medical condition those taken inside, decided to find Doctor Mike. Stack, not wanting to wait outside, joined him. They went down the same depressing halls Stack had walked earlier, looked into various rooms, and found Doctor Halpin coming out of one of them.

"How're my people?" Galoris asked. "Will they make it?"

Halpin shrugged. "If any develop a bad infection, we haven't enough antibiotics to treat them. And sometimes there are complications during operations. I can't tell yet. I'm no surgeon. And they're not the only ones with bullet-wound problems. Two fellas just brought in a guy who was shot up as bad as some of your people. I asked how it happened and they seemed to have a bit of a problem telling me. One said it was an accident. The other claimed it was an unknown assailant. They're still with him." Then the doctor headed off to continue with his rounds, but called back in a weary voice, "I've got to go see about some more sick people."

Stack looked at Galoris. "You thinking what I'm thinking?"

"Yeah."

"Let's take a look at the car those two guys drove up in." They hurried outside and went over to the dented, scratched-up vehicle. Inside, on the floor behind the front seat, they saw a shotgun and a Lee-Enfield rifle like the ones they found back at the combat site.

"That does it," Stack said. "Those two bastards are from the same gang that attacked our people. Let's go find them." As they were going back into the stadium, Worrell and Rough Trade were coming out. Stack and Galoris confronted them. Stack said to Worrell, "We're looking for a guy named Yahzdi. Ever heard of him?"

Worrell, a wary look on his face, eyed Rough Trade, then Stack. "Who's this Yahzdi?"

"Do you know him or not? I've got a message for the guy."

"From who?"

"The Tooth Fairy."

A cautious smile crossed Worrell's lips. "Which Tooth Fairy? There are lots of Tooth Fairies in Frisco. Or at least there were before the bombings," he said with a laugh, and glanced at Rough Trade, who also laughed. Then he looked at Stack and Galoris. They weren't laughing.

Worrell and Rough Trade tried to move past them, but the other men wouldn't budge. "I think you'd better stay," Stack told him. "The authorities would like your report on the circumstances surrounding your friend's wounds—" Before Stack could continue, Worrell swung a fist at him. Stack moved back, but the unexpected thrust caught him on the left side of his face. He went back still further as an "ooof" was torn from his pursed lips.

Worrell's sudden move was emulated by Rough Trade, who sent a hard right, then a left ramming into Galoris's midsection. The other man doubled up, gasping, while his heart felt as if it was going to rocket up through his throat and out his mouth. Red in the face, he folded almost in half, his arms rising to his midsection, leaving him open as Rough Trade brought a knee up and rammed it into Galoris's face. His nose exploded with red, both his nostrils jetting blood out across his chest and the floor, while he felt blood running down his throat. And this created a fear panic that he might drown in his own blood.

Stack quickly recovered and tried to move forward, his hands formed into fists. But Worrell wasn't staying to fight. He brought one shoulder down and forward, football-style, and rammed into Stack, smashing him aside as he raced for the exit, Rough Trade doing the same. Stack and Galoris had been jammed into one another by the sudden assault as they tried to sort things out in that ramjet speed of a fist fight so they could recover and make countermoves.

But by the time they'd regained their balance, the two culprits were out of the stadium. Both men, faces flushed, fist marks across their features, blood still dripping from Galoris, running across his lips and down his chin, ran for the entrance to overtake the fleeing enemy. People who'd witnessed the assault and wondered what it was all about moved out of the way in wide-eyed, open-mouthed shock as Stack and Galoris raced past, bumping into a few people still in their path. But that couldn't be helped as they ran faster than at almost anytime in their lives and made it outside, only to be greeted by the sight of their enemies starting up their car and fleeing the area, tires screeching as they roared off into the night.

Stack stomped his foot in boiling anger. "Shit, piss, and fuck," he exclaimed as he looked at Galoris. The other man was busy wiping the blood off his face.

9

Stack and Galoris raced back into the stadium, found the room Maitlin had been taken to, shoved aside the doctor who was treating him, and began to shout questions at Maitlin.

"You're one of those who attacked our people; aren't you?" Galoris spit.

"Get these guys away from me," Maitlin cried out.

The doctor who had been shoved aside pushed back in between the two parties. "Get the hell outta here," he screamed at Stack and Galoris. "This is my patient. The man's hurt. Can't you see that?"

"That man helped attack my people," Galoris yelled, pointing an accusing finger. "Plenty of victims are dead because of what he and those with him did."

"There's no time for this now," the doctor yelled back. "Let me treat this man before he dies from shock, loss of blood, and blood poisoning."

Maitlin moved back till he touched the wall the cot had been set up against, the fear evident in his face and in eyes that were so wide the whites could be seen all around the pupils.

Doctor Halpin came running in, followed by two burly paramedics and a National Guardsman. "What the goddamn is going on here?" he yelled. Then he saw Stack and Galoris as they both turned.

"This man here," Stack hiked a thumb over his shoulder, "is one of the hooligans who attacked our

154

people. He was wounded. Two of his gang brought him in, then attacked us and fled when we confronted them.''

"That may be so,'' Doctor Halpin said, "but you can't interfere with the medical procedure here. Report this to Callister. He'll have someone question him when the patient's been attended to. I can't allow any more of this. After the patient's been patched up we'll deal further with the matter.''

His words partially soothed the two men, who cast hateful glances at Maitlin, then walked past Halpin and the others, found a stairway, and headed onto the playing field, where they found Callister still giving orders and taking reports.

He saw them and waved. "Back so soon, boys? Any good news?'' They told him what had gone down.

"Shit,'' he cursed. "Okay, leave this to me. I'll question the sonofabitch when he's been fixed up. But don't let this sidetrack you. In the military you learn never to allow side issues to take your attention from the main objective. And that objective is getting your ass back to your people and preparing a better offensive before those bastards can mount another attack. Anticipate them. Try not to let them strike the first blow. Got me?''

"Yeah, we're on our way, colonel,'' Stack said as he and Galoris raced from the stadium to their van. In less than half an hour they were back at the cellar complex, where they told everyone what new events had transpired. And then Stack asked Courtner to send motorcycle messengers to Pelf and the Russians to say that the attacks would have to go in sooner even than Stack had planned on. There would be no time to train people to use the guns. Only those with previous military experience would be used, and the attacks would have to go in immediately, if possible. They had to make their countermoves now or die!

The head of the Russian emigre group and the gays, Yusupov and Pelf respectively, were roused by those on night watch. While rubbing sleep from their eyes, they were stunned by the news they received. Stars flew in front of their eyes as adrenalin began to pump through their blood. It was time to make war! Time also to die!

Trembling, barely able to dress, each leader began rousing key people in their groups. Bodies stirred as they were wakened from deep slumber or a troubled sleep in which dreamers mumbled and fought unseen foes tormenting their nights as they had tortured their days. Some smiled as they slept. Perhaps dreaming of pleasant, sweet, hopeful days now gone. These they most hated to wake. To pull them from the light into the dark hell of the present. But they did what all commanders have learned to do.

Then they left to wait for those who had been chosen to dress. Those who had been picked felt their mouths go dry. Gongs went off inside their heads. The night suddenly became an endless, terrifying thing. Each sound from outside was imagined to be the approach of the enemy, making their move before the people now dressing could come together and make theirs.

Stack, his van loaded with guns, arrived near the Russian compound half an hour later. Galoris was with him. They went to the same debris-choked courtyard as earlier and found Yusupov, Raskalnikov, and six others waiting. Stack could not bring the van to them, so they went to the van. There, he gave each man an M-16, briefly showing them how to use it. They all had used automatic weapons before, and all rifles were fairly similar to each other. Next, he gave them ammunition and clips into which the bullets had to be loaded. He also explained about these. The AK-47 and AKM rifles they had used back in the Soviet Union employed a similar clip and loading procedure. So this was not too difficult to master. Stack then asked each of them to show him how they would use and load their rifles to make sure each man would be able to operate fairly smoothly once they went into battle. When he told Yusupov that he could command his own group, under Stack's overall supervision, the Russian nodded his agreement. Stack was glad. He wanted no command problems about who'd do this or that. There wasn't the time for prima donna battles. Each minute was of essence.

Once matters had been sorted out, Stack told the Russians to squeeze into the rear of the van. They complied, though the tensions on their faces showed the turmoil inside and the wonder about who'd be coming back down the pike after the shooting had ended.

Stack and Galoris went up front and drove to where Pelf and his people were. The ride was not a long one. The night also seemed quieter, except for distant laughter. Stack wondered what was so amusing. But after listening a few seconds, he realized the laughter didn't sound human. He sensed it came from someone among the ruins whose mind had snapped and now gave vent to the rage and fantasies and fears inside.

Stack recognized the area as he reached the other compound. When he and Galoris got out of the van, one of the night sentries spotted them and came forward. He was carrying a baseball bat that had seen better days. Not much of a defense if they were attacked by men with guns. But Stack could not worry about that now. He'd come for the two ex-military men he needed for his combat team. And his insides told him he'd need every fighter he could get.

The night guard led the two men down the familiar hall they'd been in earlier to the room at the very end where Pelf waited, Boyd and Boskert with him, all three nervously smoking, their faces strained, their eyes watchful.

As soon as Stack and Galoris entered, they nodded to everyone, then Stack told Pelf, "Sorry it has to go down this way, but circumstances won't allow us any more time."

"I understand," Pelf said. "I just hope this ends quickly and that not too many people have to be lost on our side."

"My hopes exactly. But what happens is up to the Big Guy up there." He pointed toward the ceiling and the sky beyond.

"I guess so," Pelf replied. "Though I'm not much of a believer. However, this war's been making me do some deep thinking."

"Tragedy always does. Wish I could discuss this further, but we've got to be going." He looked at Boskert and Boyd. "Come on, fellas."

They nodded and followed him as Stack and Galoris waved goodbye to Pelf. They were soon back at the van with their volunteers, whom they gave guns and ammo.

Then Stack asked everyone in the van to make room for the new additions. The Russians knew who these people were and the atmosphere in the van chilled. They made plenty of room for the pair even though it was uncomfortable for them. Whether Boskert or Boyd noticed, they gave no indication. Stack shut the rear doors, got behind the wheel, and drove back to the cellar complex, where the others waited. This was going more smoothly than he had ever hoped.

Some time earlier Yahzdi stood and watched as Rough Trade and Worrell returned, driving in a crazy, frenzied manner. And then they parked in a haphazard fashion, got out, and ran over to tell Yahzdi about the confrontation. He didn't like that at all.

"Things are moving faster than I had supposed they would," he commented.

"What should we do?" Worrell asked, looking anxiously at Yahzdi.

"The same things we are doing now, only faster. As for you and your friends," he looked briefly at Rough Trade, "I am sending you on a special scouting mission." This, Yahzdi thought, would get these two pieces of trouble out of his hair. He had already sent out three two-man patrols, telling them to look for concentrations of ten or more people around firelights. That's what he should have done with Worrell the first time. Then that prick wouldn't have tried what he had. No matter. What was done was gone. Nothing to be changed now. Only to be learned from and avoided in the future.

After Worrell and Rough Trade left, Yahzdi considered moving now that others knew where he was. But so what? He had the guns and the numbers. Let the others move. This was his territory. Fuck the world, he thought, pacing up and down, running events over and over in his mind, waiting for his forward scouts to return. He looked at his watch. It was two in the morning, Yahzdi hadn't slept in almost 19 hours. Yet, strangely, he didn't feel groggy. The tension of what was going down kept him keyed up. In his younger days, when reading about the exploits of troops, he wondered how they could fight for 30 or 40 hours at a clip. He had learned how and why when he had been a soldier in the Iran-Iraq War.

Yahzdi turned now to one of his lieutenants. "Tancredi, organize a defense of this location in case some of the people we attacked attempt another probe, like they did earlier tonight, or maybe even a small attack. Though I doubt that with all the losses they've already taken. Worrell's action was not entirely a failure."

Tancredi, a lanky, dark-haired, dark-faced man, went to do as asked. About then, his forward scouts began to come in and report on what they had seen. One had discovered the location of Pelf's group. Yahzdi had the option of leaving them alone, or attacking and wiping them out before turning on the cellar complex where Worrel had failed. He decided to do the bold thing and ordered an attack. Wipe out your enemies before they can do you in. He guessed, correctly, that the natives would get restless once the first attack went in, then combine and come down hard to destroy him and his people. Well, he was not going to make it easy for them. The actions taken tonight would decide who lived, who died, and who stayed king of the mountains.

Yahzdi sent his main lieutenant, Ismail Salamis Farouky, and twenty-four picked men to take care of Pelf's complex. Yahzdi was only sorry he couldn't be there to see the slaughter. But this time there were enough men for the mission under a commander whom he respected, had faith in, and who wouldn't fail. As they left, Yahzdi stood outside the walls of his HQ compound and wondered how this night would end. There was a tension in the air. He could almost feel death stalking. Maybe it was just his nerves, he thought. Yes, Just his nerves.

Farouky marched his men hard. Time was of the essence. Yahzdi had repeated this over and over before he left. And the people, whom Farouky had personally picked, respected him enough to do as he asked without much bitching about the pace of the man-killing march.

Farouky even named his group. The Vengeance Machine, he called them. He liked the roll of the words on his tongue. As his main assistant, he picked a short, hard, wizened man with a shaved skull, a stubbled beard, and strange, cruel eyes whom others had nicknamed Queer Eyes the first day he joined their team. The kind of character who wouldn't have found a place out in the normal world. But this was no longer the normal world. And Queer Eyes took as his main man a tough, muscled brawler named Conroy, who was better known by his appointed nickname after the tattoo on his chest. A big, sharp-clawed, open-beaked eagle holding a fluttering banner with the words Flaming Savage across it. And he liked the name with which they'd tagged him. It said things he always wanted to say in his past life. No matter. Now he was doing it all.

The force made good time. Damn good time. And reached Pelf's compound shortly after the van left. In fact, some of Farouky's people saw the weaving headlights moving off through the night. This worried him enough to send Queer Eyes and Flaming Savage out to make a soft probe of the area. They returned in 20 minutes and reported that there were people down below, but only one black guy with a baseball bat topside.

"Looks too easy. Might be a trap," Farouky commented.

"Could be the real thing," Queer Eyes said. "Why don't we grab the nigger, question him, and find out what's going down?''

"Do that, but be careful not to alert anyone.''

"Will do, chief. Don't worry," Queer Eyes answered before he and Flaming Savage went off into the darkness.

Ten minutes more passed and then, from out of the dark, as tense members of The Vegeance Machine waited, the two scouts appeared, dragging the reluctant black man along, a knife to his throat, fear in his eyes.

Everyone gathered round as Queer Eyes brought his prisoner over to Farouky. The Syrian looked him up and down with the contempt only one enemy can have for another.

"What's your name?" Farouky asked, the contempt thick in his voice.

"Larry," the black man stuttered, exhibiting a slight lisp.

"Larree," Farouky said slowly and sensuously as if expelling smoke. The others laughed. None more than Steve Palermos, who had briefly been held prisoner when Stack made his soft probe.

"Tell me, Larree," Farouky said, his voice heavy with contempt, "how many of you there are.''

"Fourteen, no, sixteen.''

"All men? No transsexuals?" The laughter grew greater. "Tell me, Larree, do you still have your balls?''

"Let's find out," Palermos said. "Let's pull off his pants and cut his cojones off—if he still has them." The laughter all around grew harder and harsher.

Cold fear-sweat covered Larry's face. He couldn't believe this was happening to him. It was almost as if this were all occuring on TV and he was looking at it from far away, unattached and unconcerned. He shook his head. Maybe the bad dream would dissipate. Maybe he'd wake up and find out the war had never happened. This can't be, he kept telling himself over and over. Just one week ago he'd been the star performer in a gay theater in downtown San Francisco, playing Frankie Fongool in *Alexander's Fagtime Band*. A comedy enjoyed by straight and gay audiences both. And just before that he'd appeared in a fairly successful straight play, "Young In Utah." He'd been hired for that job after taking over as substitute in another play, "Not Tonight, Darlene." And now he was here in the hands of Neanderthals.

"What do you want from me? I've done you no harm."

"Sure, princess," Farousky spat. "No harm. All you do is spread AIDS. Lots and lots of AIDS."

"I don't have AIDS."

"You hear that, boys? Princess here has no AIDS." He looked back at Larry. "How you gonna prove it to us? Maybe you lie to save your ass."

"No, no."

"I don't care, princess. You're just shit to me. Shit to all of us. I just want to know one thing. How many queers with guns you got down in that cellar?"

"None."

"You lyin'."

"No, no. That's the truth," Larry said in a trembling voice.

"He won't talk," Farouky announced as he turned to a tall, gangling man by the name of Glendenning. "You've been boasting how good you are with a knife." Farouky pulled Larry from the grip of the two men who'd brought him in and shoved his prisoner toward Glendenning. "Show us how you carve a turkey."

Glendenning smiled, brought a foot-long hunting knife out of the sheath on his belt, and advanced on Larry. The night soon filled with shrieks and screams that ended in gurgling cries, then there was stillness. Down in his room, Francis Pelf put down his coffee, listened, and wondered what that was. One of his people? He'd send someone up to look.

At the same moment, Farouky looked down at the bleeding body of Larry, entertainer turned night guard. His corpse, pierced in many places, leaked blood like a rusty, old radiator.

"Good," Farouky said as he smiled at Glendenning. "One less queer to worry about. He was trying to sell me some jungle jive. Lying that his people have no protection. But I showed him I was no fool.''

He grinned a wide, toothy grin at his men, who beamed smiles back his way, then led his force toward the bunker where the gays were holed up, hoping against all hope that they hadn't heard Larry's cries.

He moved swiftly, eyes alert, hands tight around his gun. It was now a time of judgment. There would come a day when people would thank Ismail Farouky for what was being done here tonight.

Right behind him Queer Eyes grinned at Flaming Savage. ''A week ago they could've hung us for the homicide we're goin' to commit tonight.''

''This ain't no homicide,'' Flaming Savage replied, his voice sly. ''This is homocide.''

''Yeah,'' Queer Eyes said with a laugh as he caught the difference. ''Yeah, homocide.''

The Vengeance Machine grew deathly still as they came closer to the underground living quarters the gays occupied. The only person topside, the ever-faithful Gravy Train, had been sent out by Francis Pelf to find Larry.

''Larry, honey. Where are you?'' No one answered. ''Larry?'' Another pause. ''Are you doing number two, Larry?''

Suddenly, Gravy Train's heart gave a leap as he saw the pale glint of rifles and shotguns. A lot of them. Were Stack's people, who just left, returning for some reason? Gravy Train stood there, trying to make out faces, looking for someone familiar. But a chill ran up his spine, the primitive warning sign of a less-evolved stage of our species, and he realized these were not friends.

Gravy Train turned and started back toward the cellar at a run to shriek a warning to Francis Pelf and everyone else down there. But it was too late. He'd been spotted. Louis Attaliyah, who'd been with Worrell when they attacked Galoris's people, lifted his Lee-Enfield and placed two nicely spaced rounds into Gravy Train's back. A shriek of terror flew from his mouth as he was kicked forward while each slug dug deep, filling him with blood as Gravy Train crashed into the earth face first, twitching, gasping for breath, almost unconscious, his body still fighting for life against the shock affect of what had been done to it. The first troops of The Vengeance Machine had now reached him and some of them ran over the body, heading for the cellar entrance.

Pelf heard the shots and Gravy Train's shriek of horror and knew what had occurred. He stood up suddenly, the coffee on the table in front of him tipping over, spilling hot, brown liquid across the surface, some of it dripping down onto the floor, wisps of steam passing off into the air, but none of it being noticed now.

Pelf, heart beating rapidly, ran from the room to spread the alarm, and was therefore the first to see the enemy come charging down the hallway, single file. One of them, Steven Palermos, lifted his shotgun and fired.

The sound of it going off reverberated and was magnified by the long hall. It almost covered the sound Francis Pelf made when the blast struck him squarely in the chest. He groaned, twisted to the left, then fell back against the wall behind him, slowly sinking to his knees. He stayed that way for long seconds, swaying, bleeding, his face distorted by pain, watching through the haze that covered his field of vision as the killers moved from room to room, destroying his friends and the sanctuary home they had made for themselves. And then, while they were still in the middle of the slaughter, he fell onto his face as dead as stones around him.

When the first interior shot went off, some rushed out into the halls. But most didn't have the chance, or the inclination. They tried to get under cots, behind things, backing away against walls, or just froze in what they were doing, rooted to the floor by panic shock. Even those who had rushed into the hall retreated back into the temporary sanctuary of their rooms. And all of them were caught by the advancing enemy, pairs of which broke off, as they moved forward, to enter and check out individual rooms.

Arms flew up, mouths opened in terror, screams rent the

air amid the banging of rifles and the boom of shotguns as flashes of flame lashed out at men and under beds or cots. The pellets which flew outward broke open tall glasses holding lit candles, sending shards of glass and bits of molten wax racing to all points of the compass. Elsewhere, several salvos smashed into three men cowering against the wall of their room, forcing screams from their lips as they were pierced in a hundred places. Almost immediately hands, arms, then legs lost all power and the trio slowly slid to the ground, leaving red streaks of blood and pieces of themselves glued to the wall.

The killers did not give a damn about the aftereffects and went about their work with methodical glee, glad that the talking was over and that the doing had begun as they acted out everything they had dreamed of and more.

One gay, hidden behind a wardrobe rack in his darkened room, waited knife in hand for one of the killers to enter. And one did. Glendenning. He moved carefully, looking this way and that, finally checking under the cot in one corner. It was then that the gay sprang forward and with all his might plunged the knife into Glendenning's back. Something the attacker had never believed himself capable of. But he did it. Glendenning gasped and pulled away as the blade went in—deep. The attacker let go of the knife and put a hand to his mouth, acting out the womanly role he had picked for himself in life. Glendenning, bloody froth forming on the lips of his open, gasping mouth, looked with shocked eyes at the person who had done this, then fired into the chest of his murderer. Glendenning fell dead before the gay did. But at least one of them had the satisfaction of seeing a persecutor die.

Elsewhere, the slaughtering was almost done. Palermos had caught an 18-year-old, redheaded gay who'd attempted to hide in the produce room. He brought him into the hall to show to the others.

"Look, boys, a young faglet. What do we do with 'im?"

"Shoot 'em, hang 'im. No," a voice cried out. "I have a better idea. Let's chop off his head." With that, he brought out a hatchet.

The boy began to hysterically cry and plead for mercy as they dragged him into a room, shoved his head down on a damaged desk, and held it there by the hair and ears while others pinioned his madly flailing hands and arms. Palermos grabbed the hatchet from the man who had showed it to the mob and began to hack away at the offered neck, which was pivoted sideways. The unearthly shrieks flying from the boy's mouth turned into gurglings as the hatchet severed cords in the neck and the jugular vein and gysers of blood shot up, spraying those holding him. The hatchet was not sharp or large enough to make big, deep cuts, so Palermos, in a high frenzy now, chopped again and again, opening wide slashes as bits of the voice box and cartilage fell out. The gay was strangling now, blood shooting from his open, coughing mouth while also jetting from his nostrils as his eyes danced wildly in his head at the same time as his body struggled against his enemies with gigantic ferocity of purpose in the panic one faces toward the end. With superhuman power he fought them and with superhuman power they held on, using all their strength to pinion this victim fighting for the last vestiges of life open to him. A ruthless, non-thinking struggle in which all chances of escape were now gone. No matter. The struggle continued. But they were too many, too strong, and Palermos now cut the air pipe, separating the neck still more from the head, blood spraying over everyone, hitting eyes, mouths, noses, chins, cheeks, foreheads, and hands, which had turned greasy, slippery, and slimy, yet still held on. And then there was a shuddering before the entire frame stopped fighting, relaxing slowly as the ghost was given up. With that, Palermos delivered three final strokes and severed the skull from the body. He looked around with grim satisfaction as he lifted the skull by the hair and showed the dead face to all the assembled. But for some this had been a bit much to bear. Two of them went out into the hall, found other rooms, and vomited there.

10

Stack reached the cellar complex, where everyone got out of the van and met with Courtner's people. The meeting was brief. Some hellos, some eyeballing of what the other side had to offer. Nobody was very friendly. Everyone was tense. They knew what was coming and were uncertain about what the future held. None of the three groups knew each other intimately, or trusted one another. It was a hell of a combination to go to war with. But they were going to do it anyway. There was no other choice. They lacked numbers. Stack, Courtner, and the surviving Harley-Davidson team consisted of 10 people. The Russians added 8. Then there were the 2 gays and Bathhurst. In all 21 people. Rougly half the size of the enemy they had to stalk and hunt. Exactly 8 uninjured civilians were left in the cellar complex. Stack decided that 4 of the Harley-Davidson people would be left behind to defend them. At that point, Galoris and Bushnell walked over to Stack.

"We want to be taken along so we can pay these bastards back for what they did to us," Galoris said.

"Your place is here," Stack answered. "You two don't know how to use a gun and there's no time to train you. I need people with prior experience."

"Then take us along as ammunition carriers," Bushnell said. "Surely you'll need a lot of ammo."

Stack scratched his jaw for a second and looked at Courtner. "Okay. I assume you have knapsacks. I'll show you what to load up. It'll make things easier for us. But you're both going to have to carry a hundred pounds each and do so under all sorts of fire."

"We accept that," Galoris answered for both of them. Stack then gave them a list of what he wanted in the sacks. He also made sure each man who didn't yet have an M-16 got one, plus ammunition. Then he directed that each fighter receive two grenades, and explained how to use them in case anyone there didn't yet know.

Stack then turned to Bathhurst. "This is going faster than I thought it would. Only one thing bothers me, if we build up the force guarding the people here, we won't have enough to attack the enemy base. And if we use more fighters to attack the enemy, which still won't be enough, we weaken the protection here. Four sentries aren't enough."

"It's a bitch, ain't it?" Bathhurst said. "Commanders in battle have to decide such things all the time, then keep their fingers crossed that nothing blows up in their faces. Sometimes it does, sometimes it doesn't."

Stack said nothing. He'd made his choice and would stick by it. Everyone was now ready to march. Galoris and Bushnell said their goodbyes before the civilians went downstairs and the sentries took up their positions, nervous and watchful as they hid in the rubble surrounding the perimeter.

Now that they had finished with the slaughter, the men of The Vengeance Machine moved through all the rooms, looking for loot, stepping on or over the dead bodies of their victims. Farouky took inventory of the provisions that were now theirs. A rich hoard that would come in handy over the weeks ahead when finding food would become a more and more difficult task. But he didn't spend much time looking over what was available. It was the immediate future which counted most. He began to call his men together. They had another mission to accomplish. And the sooner it was completed, the better. One thing he had learned in life, a point further emphasized by Yahzdi, was that speed in finishing each task was essential so the next barrier might be tackled and overcome before problems piled up to such an extent that one was defeated. This having been decided, he impatiently called together his men, who were more intent on looting than anything else.

The 19-man attack team headed by Stack moved as quietly as possible through the rubble fields of the city, each minute bringing them closer to the enemy citadel. Stack was the farthest ahead, serving as point man to trip up any possible ambush and save the unit from an enveloping attack. Bathhurst was 40 feet back, and 60 feet behind him came the main body split into two commands. The bikers plus Boyd and Boskert under Courtner formed one team, and then came the Russians commanded by Yusupov. Galoris was the ammunition carrier in Courtner's group and Bushnell was with the Russians.

They were making rapid progress. At least that's how it seemed to Stack. Maybe in his present, excited state events were being telescoped. Only, there wasn't the time to examine this assumption in detail.

The first sight of the enemy position, dim firelight inside ruins, appeared sooner than expected. Stack stopped a moment to make sure no one was waiting in ambush, then he started forward again. The only thing wrong with the present system, he realized, was that he had no way of signaling those behind that he was stopping so they could do the same. One practical way of doing this was light identification. But that would make them noticeable to the enemy. So Strack advanced, the distance between him and the others having shrunken somewhat.

A few minutes more and they came to within yards of the enemy compound. The fires burning inside were clearly visible, as were the silhouettes of men moving in and out. How many were there? Stack could not tell. He saw only five or six. It didn't matter. When they began to attack the enemy would have to respond and expose their position. And then they'd know whom they had to kill and where each man was located, though positions would change during the coming firefight.

Another thing which bothered Stack was that the people with him were for the most part unknowns. He could not be sure how well they would fight, how they would react under fire or work as part of a coordinated team, which they certainly weren't. All were things he could learn as the coming battle unfolded. It was not the desired lineup to go into combat with. But the war had created some hard conditions, and the actions of the people now in their sights had created choices none too attractive, so one did what one had to, using the given tools to the best possible advantage.

Stack turned around as Bathhurst approached. Stack whispered what he had seen and surmised. "Do me a favor," he added. "Take the Russians around to the other side. Spread them out. I'll do the same on this side. Then, when I begin to fire, you join in. Is that okay with you?"

"Fine, dude. I couldn't have done better myself. See you later and the best of luck." Bathhurst disappeared back into the darkness to go find the Russians. Then more time would be lost bringing the group around to the other side. Nervous flurries passed through Stack. The tension was almost unbearable. But Stack rode hard on his nerves. Time passed more slowly now. Far too slowly for Stack, listening for sounds from the rear, worried about being detected before they were ready. So far nothing had happened. With crossed fingers he hoped it would remain that way.

Bathhurst had by now reached the Russians and explained what Stack wanted as Courtner and his people moved forward. Bathhurst began to lead the Russians to their new positions. However, they were making noise. Not really a lot, but more than was permissible this close up in the deathly quiet of the ruined city. One of the forward enemy scouts by the name of Liberholtz detected them and called to Yahzdi. "I heard something. Come quick." The tension in his voice put speed into Yahzdi's steps.

Yahzdi arrived and cocked an ear. "I hear nothing."

"I heard something, I swear."

"The wind. You are too tense my friend."

Yahzdi turned to go. "Wait, I hear it again." Yahzdi turned back and listened more carefully, his ears cocked. Then he heard it and looked at Liberholtz.

"You are right. Let me go alert the others."

But Yahzdi never had the chance. Liberholtz cried out. "Halt out there. Halt and identify yourselves."

The Russians now knew they'd been heard. They stopped, as did Bathhurst, who'd been trying to get them to move more quietly. One of the Russians saw the two figures silhouetted against the faintly illuminated rubble 70 feet away, lifted his rifle, and fired twice. Lashes of fire cut the night. Liberholtz gasped and grabbed himself, then his gun clattered to the ground and he followed it forward like a felled spruce and struck the ground with a puff of dust. Yahzdi fled for the shelter of the ruins as the night exploded with shots and colored-tracer streaks. As fire flew back and forth, both forces identified oppossing positions even though most were firing blindly at foes still unseen.

"Goddamn and double goddamn," Stack cursed as things began to come apart. He looked back. Courtner's people were running forward, some of them shooting on the run. More of the enemy began to come out of the multi-passaged HQ base. Scared faces, eyes scanning the terrain for attackers, noticed incoming rounds before the men jumped behind cover and began to fire out at the advancing assault force.

"Stay low, stay low," Bathhurst screamed out at the Russians, with Yusupov and Raskalnikov shouting the same things in Russian. Two of their people, Abugov and Dubrovir, raced forward, found cover, then, using their superior night vision, began to peg shots at the enemy. Abugov fired several times at a blonde man popping into and out of sight. Each time he missed, until the last try, when he laced into the blonde target with two rounds and watched him thrash around on the ground before he died. Abugov smiled, looked at Dubrovir, and said, "Do as good, if you can.'' The boastful edge in his voice, the warrior's joy in his eyes, got Dubrovir's goat, and then he exposed too much of himself as he peered out, trying to spot targets, shooting left, right, and center. Once, he almost hit Yahzdi, who was attempting to crawl back into the ruins.

This was horrible, horrible, Yahzdi thought. He realized he should have been more expectant of an attack. All he had with him were 12 men, the rest having gone with Farouky, or out on patrol. Despite his air of caution, he had been too cocksure and thus had miscalculated. Who knew how powerful the attack force was? It had probably come from the place Worrell attacked. He should have sent Worrel back with a larger force, Instead, he had let it slide. His thoughts were now interrupted as rounds chewed into the ground to his right and left. But none of them struck him as Yahzdi slowly crawled back into the maze of ruins.

The Russians, meanwhile, were laying down heavy fire. They had hit another man and missed one more. Yusupov and Raskalnikov had gone from directing their men to joining in the firefight. Bathhurst fired a round in one man's lower chest and watched him pitch back, before he looked over at the Russians and yelled at them not to fire so wildly and to conserve ammunition and take care.

While all this was happening, a gasping Courtner and his people arrived and took up positions along the line. George Boskert and Bart Boyd moved up alongside Stack and began to fire with relish at the enemy. The overwhelmed foe now began to retreat from the perimeter outside the walls into the ruins. Yahzdi, already inside the protecting walls of the fortress, was racing down halls, gasping, the sounds of his boots echoing against the walls while the pound of his heartbeat thundered in his ears, till he made it to the inner chamber where the now untended fire still burned with hearty power. He ignored the hypnotic yellow-orange flames, grabbed his Lee-Enfield rifle, then rushed back along dark hallways open to the sky, across which faint orange and yellow lights played and along whose moisture-slicked floors his boot-shod feet clapped, till he reached the outer wall where fighting was now going on hot and heavy. Yahzdi threw himself down and like any other soldier began to peek out and fire, then hunkered down as heavy incoming fire made his life miserable. He was no longer the great commander, the leader he had planned on being. The bottom was now the top and the world was upside down.

Stack spoke to Courtner. "We've got to catch these guys from the sides and rear. Our people have to lay down heavy fire to keep the bastards pinned while some of us penetrate into the interior."

"Good idea," Courtner gasped, intending to do the penetrating in place of Stack. He pointed to three of his men. Bill Ruald, Frank Dellatore, and Lou Senker. "Come with me." When Stack saw what was happening, he said, "Wait," then called to the others on the line and quickly explained to them about the heavy fire they would be expected to lay down on his signal.

Then he turned to Courtner and nodded as he shouted out the word, "Now." In that instant a heavy hail began to fall. Chunks of brick flew through the air, forcing enemy heads and shoulders down as eyes closed in fear and Yahzdi gasped in anguish, worried that his heart would fly up out of his throat. He'd been in some very hard situations in the Iran-Iraq War, which this present nightmare brought back with full force.

While all this was going down, Courtner led his three-man force across the open space to a low wall, then over it. Now they were inside the maze. Outside, the heavy incoming fire let up. The enemy, which had been pinned down, responded with a hail of their own as pink tracers streaked the night and slugs sent plumes of dust and debris flying. While this was happening, Courtner and his men advanced slowly along deserted halls and looked into empty rooms. They reached a corner. Being the lead man, Courtner peered around it and spotted several of the defenders, including Yahzdi. He grinned back at his people. They had the enemy in a crossfire position. Just then, one of the enemy, coming down a side hall leading into that one, spotted the intruders and yelled, "Look out behind you. They're inside." He then let loose a flurry of shots.

Cournter's force backpedaled as chunks of brick were ripped from the wall. None of the rounds struck anyone, but they did get Yahzdi and the others to turn around and start firing in panic in the same direction that Courtner and his people were running.

This was heard by the attackers outside who again laid down heavy fire to prevent the defenders from moving into the maze to catch the invaders. Bathhurst and the Russians used the opportunity to move closer to the walls of the ruin, killing another defender in the process. They wanted to use their grenades, but still weren't close enough.

A Russian named Rogvin, in a rare display of bravery, ran toward the outer wall of the ruins while others threw up a ring of protective fire. On reaching the wall, he took out a grenade, pulled the pin, and threw the lethal egg over the top. Two long seconds passed before there came a blast, a fist of fire, a shower of metal, and a scream, all at the same time as one of the enemy was caught and killed.

The Russians cheered and raced to the wall and Bushnell was running after them, carrying the ammunition sack, caught up in their bravery. And following after them was Bathhurst, trying to put a damper on their enthusiasm in case anyone was hidden, waiting for their charge so he would spray them with lethal fire. He was for bravery, yes. But caution also. Only, there was no stopping them. They went through a gap in the wall. Seeing this, the men with Stack rose and ran for the same opening. Stack, with Galoris in tow, raced after them, feeling like followers and not leaders in this crazy flow. Galoris, never having known such excitement in his life, ran with hypnotized eyes after the mob, wondering why he had been against war all these years. This was nothing like the maddening horror he'd been told about. It was so good, so macho, so manly, so invigorating.

Stack and Bathhurst, who were supposed to be the aggressive leaders, were actually bringing up the rear. But they tried to move to the front as fast as their bodies and combat gear would allow them, moving at the same time with the impetus of the herd, reacting more than acting, unable to control the direction of events, which moved them along like chess pieces on a great unseen board.

Only seven of the enemy were still alive, and ran like madmen, deeper into the maze, stopping to peer around corners and send shots flying. The rounds mostly missed, streaks of fire chewing into walls. One of them struck the Russian Abugov and he was killed instantly. Still, the attackers moved on, almost fearless, unthinking bravado now their stock in trade, their feet swift and tireless across the dark floor underneath, their eyes glancing almost unseeingly as the dark walls on both sides streaked by, the mob slowing only long enough to look into each room ahead, going around corners fearlessly, foolishly, unthinkingly, not wondering about the guns possibly waiting on the other side.

Yahzdi looked back as one of his slower men tried to make it around one corner of the maze, then arched as slugs tore into his back before he fell to earth, not yet dead, as he was trampled down by the violent herd racing over him. Stack gnashed his teeth. Here he was, in the rear of everything. Not even able to get a clear shot at the enemy because of all those ahead of him. A follower and not a leader.

Yahzdi would gladly have been someplace else right then. But that couldn't be. He had to deal with the reality which existed and not the one he wanted. Like the hunted animal he was, he retreated on tireless legs, the fear within him a mighty ram which propelled him around corner after corner, deeper into the center of the maze.

His head was nearly coming part with the fear pounding inside. His eyes were wide with shock. Bright lights flew past his field of vision, tension sweat oozed from his pores, making his rifle slippery in his hands. But he held onto it for dear life. Yahzdi knew things were getting worse with each second that passed. He had to make a stand and make it now. He went around the next corner, stopped, swung around, and popped back around, letting three rounds fly

into the mass of those chasing after him. Two slugs dug
into walls, but the third struck home, catching Bill Ruald
in the mouth. He staggered back into the man behind him
as a flash of blood erupted from the lower part of his face
while his teeth went flying in all directions like Chiclets.
The bullet did not stop and lodged in the roof of his
mouth. Ruald dropped to the ground, his rifle clattering,
blood running from his mouth as he moaned in semi-conscious pain. But the men around him were too hopped up
and, except for one, did not stop, but jumped over him,
Stack joining them, no longer able to control his feelings.

Yahzdi retreated again down this hall into another. But
then he saw Bathhurst's people and Yusupov's coming in
on his right, battling the defenders on that flank. He took
an exit into another passage, moving closer to the center
where his warm room, with the fire still going, waited. This
couldn't be happening, he kept telling himself. But it was.

And soon, Allah would be standing over him. With the
acceptance of his faith and the Islamic fanaticism taught to
him long ago, he began to fight harder as two of the
remaining members of his force, Tancredi and an Arab
from Yemen, retreating from the opposite direction, came
toward him laying down a curtain of lead.

One of the Russians, Rogvin, staggered as he caught a
round in the chest, then slapped the spot where the round
had gone in and keeled over dead. The headlong charge
stopped as Russians moved out of the hall into the rooms
opening off it to pop out and fire at will. Yahzdi grunted.
The tune of battle had been changed on one flank. Now to
do the same elsewhere.

While the Yemeni and Tancredi kept up their rifle
exchange, Bathhurst and Bushnell moved up. Yahzdi
took advantage of the lull in fighting to pump rounds
Courtner's way, one of the bullets streaking into brick just
inches above Courtner's head. The biker leader responded
by dodging into the room to his left. Stack didn't do the
same. Instead, he backtracked, going past Galoris, whom
he told to stay put. But Galoris, having picked up Ruald's
rifle, followed Stack as he found another passage through

the maze and advanced carefully toward the light. Both men spotted the Yemeni, Tancredi, and Yahzdi moving into and out of view just ahead. They moved cautiously, popping into any available room, seeking temporary shelter before they advanced again. Stack wanted to be close enough not to miss when he fired. But he overplayed his hand. The Yemeni, perhaps wanting to say something to Tancredi, looked back and saw the two Americans. He swung around, shouted to the others to watch out, and fired his rifle. Stack and Galoris dodged into a room on their left. In that instant six shots rang out from the Russian position. In turning to fire at the intruders, the Yemeni had exposed his back, forgetting for one moment in the heat of battle about the other combatants, and was struck three times. His mouth became an open hole of surprise. Then, it slowly closed as he slid down the wall he had grabbed onto. His body struck the floor with a thud, sending up a puff of dust. At that moment, Stack and Galoris emerged and began to head up the hall, with the Russians and Bathhurst also coming. Then Courtner and his people began to move, all of them converging toward the center.

Tancredi attempted to stop this, swinging left, right, then back around, not knowing which way to turn, while Yahzdi jumped into a nearby room, which he exited through a gap in the opposite wall. Meanwhile, Tancredi began to fire, but caught no one as answering rounds pierced him front and back.

The opening he had given Yahzdi was used by the Iranian, who fled to the temporary safety of the room where the great fire burned and into which there was only one entrance. Here he waited, desperate, armed, scared. The night, for him, grew many degrees colder. A faint humming began inside him and soon passed all through his body so that it affected his vision, causing everything in his field of view to dance as if it was made out of small, individual balls. He looked down. His gun also wiggled in his hands like a snake suddenly come to life. But he held onto it. The Lee-Enfield was his life now. His eyes remained on the open doorway, his right shoulder pressed against the wall to the right of the entrance, the warm fire along his sides giving him that secure glow fires always give men. Only this time he felt the flames of hell licking at him. But now there was no more time to think.

Outside, Stack moved up the hall, all eyes on him, everyone holding his breath. He moved till he reached the entrance, experiencing a faint feeling of déjà vu as his memory transported him back hours earlier to when he had stood alone at this spot, peering into a room full of men with guns. Now there was only one man and no sounds of merriment.

Stack let part of his face slip briefly past the corner so he could peer in, ready to immediately pull back if there was a rifle waiting for him. But there was none. He saw part of the room, the roaring fire, the dancing reflections of flames across the walls and a shadow. Yahzdi's. Long, pale, and sinister across the floor, wall, and ceiling. It told him Yahzdi's position. Stack pulled back and nodded to Bathhurst that he knew their man was inside and where. At the same time, Stack took out one grenade, pulled the pin, and let the tongue arm go. Then he counted one-one thousand and two-one-thousand before he swung around the corner, throwing the grenade left-handed, though he was a righty, and quickly pulled back and closed his eyes.

Yahzdi sucked in air so fast he hissed at the sight of the flying egg. Lethal death coming his way. The egg tumbled end over end before landing at the edge of the fire. Yahzdi did not wonder if the licking flames would cause it to go off faster as he staggered back until he hit the corner just behind him and dropped his gun, throwing his arms up to defend his face, bringing his head down almost to his chest while his eyes screwed shut and his face wrinkled in fearful expectation in those brief seconds before the nightmare to come. He began to sink down now. But his time was up.

The grenade exploded quite suddenly, the sound of it reverberating off the walls of the room, then whooshing up into the open air and the night sky. The explosion, an elongated, ugly ball of brief, red fire two yards across, fringed by blackish smoke, came apart on waves of pin-sized shrapnel which chewed first into the fire, tossing the flames five feet higher for one brief flash of eternity, and causing hundreds of orange sparks to dance into the air on a pillar-shaped puff of grayish smoke. Simultaneously, shrapnel chewed into the surrounding walls and also the cowering, sinking Yahzdi, biting into his midsection, legs, groin, and arms, which fell away as a gasp was torn from his mortally wounded body. And when his arms fell down, the shards pierced his face, which leaked blood from dozens of holes, ripped at his hair, forced his eyes to bulge open, and burned all the hairs from his arms as Yahzdi finally fell down dead.

Nick Stack, followed by Galoris and the others, rushed in and checked the corners of the room, his M-16 ready. But it wasn't needed. Aside from the crackle of the flames, the room was silent. Stack went over to the huddled, bloody mess that represented Mohammed Yahzdi and kicked it a few times to see if it moved. It didn't. He turned around as Bathhurst came into the room. Several of the men there put cigarettes in their mouths and bent over to light them off the still-burning fire.

Stack looked at Bathhurst and Courtner. "We'd better check out the entire complex to make sure no one is hiding on us. Then we'll gather up the guns and ammo, which should come in handy. This isn't over by a country mile. There are more of these bastards around."

It was then that they heard the sounds of gunfire. Distant gunfire. They hadn't heard the shooting in Pelf's bunker because it had been too far away and underground. But this was topside and Bushnell recognized the distance and direction.

"They're attacking our compound," he yelled.

"Quick. Let's get the hell back there," Galoris shouted. All thoughts of searching the ruins and picking up guns and ammo were forgotten now. They had to return to their base on the double. Yusupov, in rapid, staccato Russian, was already giving his men their orders.

Stack cursed under his breath. Now he knew where the rest of the enemy was.

11

Ismail Salamis Farouky had ordered the placing of his men
around the enemy perimeter and, after a brief period of
observation, guessed about the hidden sentries and judged
that they could take this place. All that was now needed
was for some of his men to expose themselves by firing
randomly into the perimeter, then hunkering down, letting
the enemy sentires expose themselves as they were tricked
into giving counterfire. When it came, he was surprised
how close they were—in one case only five yards from one
of his hidden men. And he was further surprised by how
few there were. This would be a piece of cake.

Louis Attaliyah fired first. His shots sliced through the
blackness. Then, as the echoes died away, there was no
answering fire for long seconds, as if the defenders did not
want to believe this was happening. But that was not the
real reason. The four sentries, forming a diamond-shaped
defense perimeter, with each man being one point of the
diamond, were trying to ascertain from where the shot had
come. Then one more shot and another came from
Farouky's people, and answering fire finally came from
inside the perimeter as the sentries picked the spots from
which the shots had originated. Raussenbush, Stu
Englund, Vance Chickering, and Cy Boozerton laid down
a smattering of fire that struck no one since the attackers
hunkered down, letting the defenders expend their initial
thrust before rising up and letting them have hell.

Each of the sentries realized independently it was impossible to stay topside. Between letups in the firing, as the attackers reloaded, the defenders started to make runs from behind one barrier to the next in an attempt to get to the cellar complex. Each of them wondered what would have happened had the bulk of their people not gone off to attack the enemy HQ. But they had the present reality to deal with and not the hoped-for-best-case scenario. Each of the retreating sentries hoped and prayed that their people had heard the din of the attack and were on their way back. But hoping wouldn't save them now. Only prayer and fleetness of foot as they retreated from behind one spot to the next as shots followed and sometimes preceeded them. Raussenbush didn't even try to see what had happened to his dropped rifle. He joined the others in their final run for the dubious safety of the underground cellars. They ran as swiftly as possible, praying that the cover of darkness would make them harder to hit. And to further insure their safety, the three men with guns fired their M-16s on full automatic, spraying the area around in arcs of prophylactic fire to make the enemy hunker down, or at the very least cut into their accuracy. A man being fired at is seldom very accurate. One watches one's ass and is not very concerned with kicking the other man's butt.

Their attempt was only partly successful. Raussenbush caught a round in the right calf, yelled, and went down. Cy Boozerton, at great risk to himself, turned, grabbed Raussenbush by the left wrist, and, with all the super-human power men in battle have, dragged him along the ground. Raussenbush, by now greatly excited and afraid, felt almost no pain as he was dragged over rough ground while his badly damaged calf sprinkled blood all over the place.

Down in the cellar, the half-dozen civilians wondered what was going on above and huddled together. Joy Church among them, telling everyone to pray to God, to stay calm, and that all would be well—though she didn't believe it.

And then, suddenly, the defenders from above burst into the cellar, one of them dragging Raussenbush, whose wounded leg bumped along the steps going down. He was unceremoniously dropped. Vance Chickering then ran back to the entrance and attempted to peer out. But his attempt only drew hellfire. A look of shocked horror was written across his features as he pulled back.

Seeing that all opposition had ended topside, Farouky rose and, rifle in the air, like on those PLO posters he had seen enough of in his life, called out to his men to advance, then led the charge to the cellar entrance.

As the horde advanced out of the ruins, Chickering looked out again, saw them coming, and let loose a dozen shots. Two men went down, one dead before he hit the ground, the other wounded. This put a temporary damper on the charge and the men of the Vengeance Machine dropped down and waited, while a pair of fighters went to see about the two who had been felled, pulling the wounded one aside so they could minister to him.

Chickering, panicking now, moved back from the entrance, shouting, "They're going to charge soon. We can't hold them. Quick, down into the tunnel."

Without question, everyone headed for the lower cellar, with Boozerton helping Raussenbush, who had an arm around Boozerton's neck while he kept one leg in the air and hopped with the other, each hop sending a spasm of purple fire through him. But Raussenbush bore the pain. War calls its own tune and all must march to its drummer.

Chickering brought up the rear, moving to the lower cellar as the first of the enemy, Cowboy Bob, came down the stairs cautiously, peering into a dimness lit only by a dying firelight. Chickering turned, saw the intruder, and fired twice, wildly. Cowboy Bob rushed back up the stairs as slugs struck brick and rock, missing him completely.

Chickering now retreated into the next cellar, spotting his friends as they moved through the hole in the wall to the right. This was the final defense, as well as an endless escape tube which led to who knew where.

Joy Church, in the tunnel with the rest of them, looked fearfully at the weak light streaming into the sewer, which was cooler than the outside world and pitch black, so that one couldn't see one's hand in front of one's face. The distant echo of a wind smelling strongly of the sea whipped past. It raised goose pimples on some skins. But most, including Joy Church, sweated with the tension of the moment, making their faces hot to the touch.

Cowboy Bob, advancing more cautiously now, looked down into the cellar again, saw no one, and began descending the stairs, each man coming after him, single file, each using the one in front as a shield. Cowboy Bob may not have realized it, but jumping back now, if anyone fired, would be impossible. There were too many blocking plugs behind him. But that was not what he was thinking of. The waves of war had him by the short hairs and drove him with that rhythm of men in battle which those who have never fought cannot understand when they attempt to rationalize why men do dangerous and horrible things in combat.

At the other end of the cellar complex, Chickering was the last into the tunnel. "Everybody here?" he asked in a tense voice sounding strange in that atmosphere and with those acoustics.

"Everybody," one of the sentries replied. Chickering did not even recognize the voice.

Inside the first cellar, the enemy moved slowly, eyes carefully scanning every detail, tense hands on ready guns, worried faces wondering where the enemy was and if there was a trap and when it would be sprung.

They moved through the room, then Cowboy Bob carefully looked into the cellar beyond. It was full of sacks of stuff, but not people. Maybe they were hiding among the sacks. He fired randomly in a wide arc, and then pulled back to see if he could draw fire and get the enemy to reveal their positions. But all he did was put holes in some sacks and send wet chunks of potatoes flying.

He peered out again and still saw nothing, while the man

behind them held their guns at the ready. And then Cowboy Bob advanced into the room, eyeballing every corner, super-aware, spotting the hole in the wall and moving toward it. He reached the opening and cautiously looked in. Now he was silhouetted in the weak light from outside. Chickering found the offer too good to refuse.

He lifted his rifle, aimed, and fired twice. The rounds winged their way across the gap between the two men in a short, single spurt, striking Cowboy Bob in the face, mangling and disfiguring him as they dug deep. He went back with a groan that quickly turned into gurgling as he dropped to the floor, his rifle clattering on the concrete, the sound of it echoing and mixing with the sounds of the expended rounds, the smell of the fired powder mingling with the sea smell in the tunnel. Cowboy Bob, not yet dead, thrashed about on the floor. Chickering could not guess how close to death he was and didn't really give a damn. Not after all the things that those bastards had done.

Outside, the enemy hid behind sacks and looked at each other. Farouky, who had advanced into the room, said to one of his people, "Pull him out." The man, a heavy-set Iraqi Arab, hesitated only momentarily and went to do as ordered, grabbing the wounded man by the ankles and pulling him back. The Cowboy continued thrashing about, but very weakly.

Chickering peeked out, saw this, and fired. Four slugs rammed into the body on full automatic. Cowboy Bob danced a moment, then all the life in him fled. The Iraqi dropped his legs and retreated behind a nearby line of sacks. He looked back at Farouky.

"He's dead," the Syrian announced. "Our problem now is how to get into the next chamber without losing our necks." He decided to take the initiative. A leader couldn't send his men to do everything.

Farouky moved slowly toward the opening, glancing briefly at the dead Cowboy Bob, then carefully started to peer in. Chickering spotted him and began firing, but too soon. The Syrian pulled back as chunks of concrete began to fly from the edge of the hole.

He jumped behind some sacks and called back to a few of the nearer men, "This part will not be easy. There is no other way in that we know about. And, as long as they keep the entrance under fire, they can prevent us from taking them."

This, he realized, was almost a Mexican standoff.

Above ground, Stack and his force were approaching, moving more slowly now, their eyes and ears alert like never before. The sounds of gunplay and flashes of fire they had seen from afar had now disappeared. This bothered Stack. It could mean the enemy attack was successful and that now everyone was dead, or, in some cases, captured and taken away. But then he heard gunfire. Faint. Sporadic. And coming from below. That meant the enemy had penetrated the defense perimeter and was now inside. He turned, looked for Bathhurst, and motioned him over. Galoris and Courtner also came forward and, in a quick conference, Stack told them his suspicions.

"The only way we'll really know is by going inside," Galoris said.

"Fine," Stack agreed. "But first, let me do a quick circuit to make sure no ambush has been prepared for us. Let's just hope that none of our people, if they're topside, mistake us for the enemy and accidentlly shoot at us." They all nodded agreement, and Stack disappeared into the darkness.

He went faster than was wise, with less caution than he would ordinarily employ, as he made a swift circuit of the area. While doing so, he spotted Raussenbush's smashed gun, and saw one of the enemy wounded writhing in agony as two of his compatriots tried to comfort him while saying all would be well. The cellar complex was definitely in the hands of the enemy. But where were the sentries? Had they been killed, he would have seen bodies topside. He didn't think they would have run off, even had they wanted to. The enemy attack pattern, as revealed once before, was to surround and then attack from all sides. That meant the sentries had to be downstairs. And, judging from the sporadic shooting below, they were still putting up a struggle.

Stack returned and told the others what he had heard and seen. Then they planned their attack. An approach from two sides, with two pairs of scouts going first. Stack and Courtner would be in Team One. Bathhurst and Yusupov would be in the second team.

Everything decided, the two combat teams separated and approached from opposite directions, angled toward each other. As they emerged from the rubble, one of those ministering to the wounded man on the ground spotted them and yelled a warning to his friend as he grabbed for his shotgun. He never made it. Bathhurst opened up on full automatic, caught the clump of men, and killed all three, not distinguishing between armed, unarmed, or wounded.

Stack wanted to say that they had the drop on the enemy and that this wasn't necessary and that men shouldn't kill unless there was absolutely no choice. But the momentum of war was upon them now. There wasn't the time for moral discussions.

Below, the members of The Vengeance Machine heard the gunfire, and it told them that while they were trying to put a cork on the people in the tunnel, a bigger cork was being placed on the bottle they were in. Would the easy victories end now? Would this place be their tomb? Shivers of fear raced through some. But Farouky wouldn't be fazed by anything.

"Quick," he said to five men he picked at random. "Go back and see if you can get out. If not, block the entrance. Lay down a curtain of fire and call for help."

They ran to do his bidding and quickly found out the score. As they reached the entrance steps, they spotted Stack coming down. In shock and surprise they hesitated a fraction of a second. He didn't and opened fire on full automatic. Hot bees of steel swarmed across them, knocking first two, then the rest of the group down. They fell in agony, bleeding like stuck pigs, two dead, the rest wounded as Stack backtracked, trying to get the hell out of there.

At the same time as Farouky led a force toward the entrance, Stack told Bathhurst what was up. "Let me lead this one in," Bathhurst said. "Everybody behind me. As soon as you're off the stairs, spread out, then feed 'em all the lead and grenades they can eat."

Courtner fell in behind him. Boskert and Boyd jumped in line next, then the rest of the Harley-Davidson people, followed by the Russians, Bushnell, and Galoris. The last two wanted to be among the first, but were not aggressive enough in grabbing a spot on the line.

Downstairs, Farouky was stunned by the carnage. He had six men with him and seven more in the other cellar blocking off the tunnel. Farouky held back and called to the fallen men. Two were conscious and answerd him, saying they were injured and asking Farouky to come help.

He started toward them, the others bringing up the rear, when racing down the steps came the cursing form of Bill Bathhurst, already firing on full automatic before he even hit the bottom of the stairs. Farouky began to fire, lifting his rifle, trying to work the bolt, aim, and pull the trigger at the same time, learning firsthand the great drawback of bolt-action rifles versus the modern non-bolt automatics which Bathhurst and those coming down behind him and spreading out were now swinging left, right, and back again.

Farouky's bullets, too few and far between, badly aimed, flew in different directions, ate into walls, sent sparks and chunks flying. Bathhurst's rounds in those seconds of swift action were better aimed and more numerous as they chopped into Farouky's chest. With an audible "ooof," his arms flew out, his back arched, he twisted to the left, his chest expanded, his rifle dropped from suddenly limp fingers, and then he dropped back. The man behind him, also caught by the major's rounds, staggered back. But the third man bringing up the line was simultaneously able to fire off his double-barrel shotgun. The sound of the blasts echoed as the fiery eruption thrust pellets upward, catching a number of the charging rescuers, including Bathhurst, who attempted to dodge the blast, but took a nice number of pellets in the upper right chest anyway! All these things happened in fractions of seconds. The same pellet shower that struck Bathhurst also hit Courtner and some of the Russians on the stairs, though they were trying to spread out and move away from the line of fire. Stack, shielded by those in front of him, ran left, then dropped to the floor and, from his prone position, began firing on full automatic, adding to the hornets of metal being sent out by both sides, piercing the shadowed semi-darkness with streaks of flame that missed their target more often than they struck home.

All of this was occurring in mini-seconds while each player in the intricate ballet of death continued to act out his part in the overall scene. Bathhurst, wounded by the blast, began to fall, dropping his rifle, his wounds leaking blood over everything. Stack, caught up in his own deadly horror, noticed almost nothing, his finger glued to the trigger of his rifle, which spewed out a deadly tattoo as he fired his entire thirty-round clip at one go, the bullets zinging out from his ground-level vista, tearing open legs and stomachs. But the enemy did not only take, it gave. One Russian caught in an orgy of flying metal, went down screaming. At the same time fire from the attacking side continued to tear into the foe.

A Russian pulled the pin on his grenade and threw it so that the egg sailed over the heads of the few enemy fighters still left and now retreating, behind a curtain of protective fire, toward the sanctuary of the other cellar. But the grenade was swifter. It landed behind them and exploded in a dirty, red ball which sent shrapnel chopping into the surprised enemy, opening them in a hundred places as they folded to the floor, bleeding profusely, dying, or already dead.

Chickering and the others in the tunnel heard the racket out front and realized their prayers had been answered. Help had arrived. The people in the tunnel took heart.

"Come on, boys," Chickering cried out as he moved to the hole in the tunnel wall. Two sentries joined him. Raussenbush, conscious, but in great pain, smiled at them through gritted teeth.

The enemy in the lower cellar now raced to the entrance of the room and peered out at the invaders spreading across the upper cellar, their forms illuminated by a dying fire in one corner. Louis Attaliyah did not wait for anyone to tell him what to do. He advanced into the upper room and began to fire with fierce desperation. Men dropped behind cover, while Sack, still on the floor, tried to hit him. One of the Russians caught a round in the side as he attempted to race behind a pillar. Two others made it out of view, jumping over the dead and wounded. Theirs and the enemy's.

Attaliyah jumped behind an obstacle as Stack attempted to eject an empty clip and insert a new one. It was also time for Attaliyah to change clips, then he peered out and fired, catching Lou Senker, one of the bikers, in the chest. The bullet penetrated into the left lung. Senker went down spitting blood. But that was Attaliyah's last successful hit. Stack opened up and ripped his head off with a well-aimed volley, then rose and by example led the others toward the lower cellar.

It was then that he heard shooting from the other room. Chickering and Dellatore, each taking one side of the hole in the tunnel wall, had started hammering out at the half-dozen men trapped in indecision between the two forces. How dark and harsh the night had turned. From easy victory to swift death.

One of the hooligans caught five slugs in the back as half the remaining force turned their guns on the tunnel opening while the others held off the invaders from above. The sudden assault killed Dellatore and sent Chickering skittering back away from the flying slugs and endless chips of dancing concrete.

Just then Stack peered around the corner of the entranceway into the lower cellar, extended his rifle, and fired a long burst which sent bullets tumbling through the air, cutting open sacks, sending wet slivers of potatoes flying as one of the remaining invaders, Steve Palermos, caught a handful of slugs in his upper back and the rear of his skull. In a burst of red droplets, he screamed to the heavens as his hands went flying to his head before he dropped down between the sacks as dead as any man can ever be.

The others, some of whom had been looking back at where Chickering was, took cover, though one showed enough guts to pop up and fire his shotgun at Stack, who pulled back while pellets ate into the concrete where his head had been seconds before.

But the enemy was finished. The technological edge was with Stack and his men. Stack looked back and screamed to his people, "Grenades. I need grenades."

"Here," Bathhurst offered, using his good arm to extend a grenade. Others, including Bart Boyd, offered their grenades.

"Thanks, boys," Stack said, taking the lethal eggs from them. Putting down his rifle, he pulled the pin from the first grenade, let the tongue arm fly up, extended his arm past the edge of the entrance, and threw with all his might. He quickly followed with a second grenade, then a third.

Chickering, who was only now again trying to peer out of the hole in the tunnel, saw what was going down and pulled back. In the room full of so many potato sacks the remaining invaders saw the first grenade coming and hunkered down once more.

The egg went off in a flash of fire and flying steel. Not close enough to kill, but near enough to wound one of the enemy, who jumped up howling. That set him up for the second flying egg, which crucified him in a globe of burning steel. Then came the third grenade, which landed atop a sack of potatoes, blew up, and sent pieces of burning burlap and chunks of shattered spuds raining down on everything. Just then, Chickering began to fire into the room. The remaining three men, frantic now, tried to turn and fire at him, the echo of the explosions still ringing in their ears. At that moment, Stack, waving to the men behind him to join in, charged into the lower cellar firing in bursts as he moved his gun, left, right, and center. Boskert, Boyd, and Yusupov came running after him, guns blazing.

The survivors of the Vengeance Team did not even have time to turn around and look at their attackers before each was pierced by half a dozen or more slugs and then dropped down, bleeding onto the sacks of potatoes.

An ecstatic Chickering, leading the survivors of his group out of the tunnel, was embraced by a mildly wounded Bay Courtner, who staggered in from above. Others also embraced, tears in some eyes. The war was over. They'd won.

Stack ran into the other room, past cheering men patting him on the back, including Galoris and Bushnell, whose ammunition they hadn't needed after all. He ran till he reached Bathhurst and knelt down.

"You okay, trooper?"

Breathing hard, Bathhurst answered, "Nothing that a good surgeon can't cure, thought it means I'll be side-tracked a while and won't be able to do any recovery work or find my family." His voice broke at the end.

"I'll find them for you."

Bathhurst's eyes misted. "You'd do that?"

"Look at all you did. It's the least I can do to return the favor. Now rest easy. I'll get the van so you and the other wounded can be taken to Candlestick Park. We'll also have to go back to enemy HQ to pick up Bill Ruald and the man we left behind to tend him till this was over."

"You can handle the job," Bathhurst said with a grin.

"I guess so," Stack said with a laugh. "I've become a pretty good ambulance driver with all the wounded I've had to deliver." Bathhurst coughed and nodded. He looked a lot older, weaker, and less intimidating now.

Someone called to Stack, who told Bathhurst he had to leave, but would be back. The man who had called, Bay Courtner, stood against a pillar and began talking about the need to form up burial details to dispose of the numerous dead. Stack nodded while watching Galoris in one corner with Joy Church. They were embracing. She was sobbing on his chest, talking softly, telling him what was in her heart. He was patting her on the back, a distant, faraway look in his eyes.

Suddenly, Stack wasn't hearing Courtner any longer. His gaze swept across the dead, the wounded, the unharmed as he sniffed the scent of dead men and expended cordite. What a filthy hell war was.

Worrell and Rough Trade, returning to their HQ from their scouting mission, had seen and heard the battling at various points and assumed that it was their people who were winning. But, on approaching their base, Worrell scented something was wrong. Then he saw the men in the ruins. One was wounded, the other was ministering to him. But these weren't his people. He whispered that to Rough Trade.

To make sure, they skimmed the perimeter, then penetrated into the interior and headed along familiar halls, past empty rooms, and over the bodies of men they had known, penetrating to the inner chamber, where they found a dead and bloody Yahzdi. No one had to tell them what had happened.

"We've lost," Worrell gasped.

"What do we do now?"

"We can do two things. Join the dead, or save ourselves. Now let's get the fuck outta here." With that, Tim Worrell led the way out of the HQ maze as he and Rough Trade sought safety among the darkness and silence of the ruined city.